Also by Dathan Belanger

Historical Fiction

The Faith of a Centurion

Clean Forgotten Patriots:
In the American War of Independence

Alternate Fiction

The First Revolution Series

Book One: The Rise of the Reprobi

ANGELS
—AND—
MIRACLES
ON THE BATTLEFIELD

DATHAN BELANGER

CLAY BRIDGES
PRESS

Angels and Miracles on the Battlefield

Copyright © 2021 by Dathan Belanger

Published by Clay Bridges in Houston, TX
www.claybridgespress.com

eISBN: 978-1-68488-008-9
ISBN: 978-1-68488-009-6 (Paperback)
ISBN: 978-1-68488-010-2 (Hardback)

Special Sales: Clay Bridges titles are available in wholesale quantity. Please visit www.claybridgesbulk.com to order 10 or more copies at a retail discount. Custom imprinting or excerpting can also be done to fit special needs. Contact Clay Bridges at Info@ClayBridgesPress.com.

TABLE OF CONTENTS

PREFACE

President Woodrow during WWI, also called the Great War, said the war would "make the world safe for democracy" to help justify the Americans' declaration of war on Germany as a way to protect human freedom. The great promise, "This is a war to end all wars." President Woodrow Wilson gave this quote in 1917, leading the world to hope that human nature could actually change. He was not the first to say this. The writer H.G. Wells, known for *The War of the Worlds*, invented the phrase. He predicted in his article titled "The War That Will End War," published in *The Daily News* on Aug 14, 1914, that WWI would be the last of the great wars.

WWI was not a war to end all wars. What went wrong? Why do we still have war? George McGovern, a Democratic Party presidential nominee in the 1972 election, said, "I'm fed up to the ears with old men dreaming up wars for young men to die in." History might as well be a wave crashing on the shore, for men have learned nothing, but how to fill a grave. Albert Einstein may have said it best with his quote, "So long as there are men, there will be wars. It may be in our nature to destroy ourselves. However, there is hope. That is if we can understand empathy to 'Love the neighbor as yourself' (Leviticus 19:18)."

I wrote this book so readers could experience a fascinating story and learn details of history they would not normally gain from a typical history book or academic text. I firmly believe in the value of historical fiction. These novels use fun stories to show how circumstances affected people personally, deeply, and emotionally, but also how our history directly contributed to our growth and betterment of society. Historical fiction not only tells us what happened, but it makes us feel; it elicits empathy for what our ancestors experienced in difficult times. Learning the truth of history is important, even if you don't like what you learn. Not all history is beautiful, but it does not mean it should be canceled. It takes great effort and courage to seek the truth and not be guided or influenced by negative emotions and prejudices. I hope that readers will come to understand a little more about WWI through the trials that took place at the front, the fighting that took place right up to the end, and the story of angels that may walk the battlefields.

The timeline of this novel takes you through the war from the American and German perspectives. You will visit the war from the American perspective with Private Myles Archambault, a naive youth with patriotic fervor just out of high school, and from the German perspective with Company Commander Franz Fischer, a loyal Jew fighting for his fatherland. You will witness their trials and suffering and walk with them as they try to make sense of the reality of war versus their expectations.

This book will share a perspective that is widely believed by many, that there is a supernatural intervention in times of war. There is evidence of angels and divine visions influencing battles. There have been countless documented eyewitness reports from groups of soldiers and individuals. One of the earliest accounts involved The Battle of the Milvian Bridge between the Roman Emperors Constantine I and Maxentius on 28 October 312, in which Constantine reported that he had a vision: "The Christ of God appeared to him with the sign which had appeared in the sky and urged him to make himself a copy of the sign which had appeared in the sky, and to use this as a protection against the attacks of the enemy."— Eusebius of Caesarea, *Life of Constantine*, 1.29

God's divine intervention during WWI was especially relevant because this conflict seeded WWII. Two important historical events arose out of these wars, and without them they might not have happened. A direct result of allied victory in the First World War was the Balfour Declaration that established a home for Jews in Palestine. Arising out of the Second World War was the creation of the State of Israel. These two events are still having their impact upon the world, and an even greater impact is still to come.

INTRODUCTION

The Great War, so titled because it was thought to be the last of its kind, bloodied Europe. Great masses of youth were conscripted to serve their nations and provide the blood. The British Empire and the French Third Republic were currently locked in a stalemate with the German Empire at the Western Front. The British Expeditionary Force was looking to break this stalemate with the recent introduction of a multitude of men who had volunteered for army service at the outbreak of the war in 1914 and 1915 and had just finished training. This included dutiful men who had joined neighborhood infantry battalions—made up of relatives, workmates, and friends from the same community. This advance would herald the first major battle of Europe fought by a large citizen volunteer army rather than professional soldiers. Although the new volunteers did not have battlefield experience, British command thought overwhelming numbers and careful planning would win the day. They planned the Battle of the Somme that would take place on both sides of the upper reaches of the River Somme in the Picardy region of Northern France with the intent to destroy the German army and end the war swiftly.

Before the advance, the Allies launched a week-long unceasing artillery bombardment, firing some 1.75 million shells, which they thought would destroy the German defenses. On the morning of July 1, 1916, eleven divisions of the British army, most of them volunteers, began advancing on a 15-mile front north of the Somme. To further destroy the German defenses at their weakest point, 5 French divisions advanced on an eight-mile front to the south. The heavy artillery barrage, mostly shrapnel shells, barely damaged the German defenses. The shells failed to penetrate the deep holes and concrete bunkers the Germans were hiding in and almost 30% of the rounds failed to explode.

Immediately after the barrage ended the British troops attacked in long, close-formed lines. The German defenders emerged and mowed down the advancing lines of British troops with deadly fire. By the end of the day, the German defenders had inflicted one of the most murderous defeats on any army. British forces suffered 19,240 troops killed and 57,470 casualties on the opening day of the battle alone. In Britain's military history this was their single most disastrous day. The Allied forces were led like sheep to a slaughter. This disastrous offensive should have been halted, but Allied command wouldn't quit, and they continued to slug it out with the Germans with terrible casualty numbers. In October, the Allies were painfully pushing forward until wet weather hampered their advance, with troopers fighting muddy land as well as German artillery and fighter planes. Early November, the last assault on the German positions by the Allies took place within the Ancre River valley. With winter approaching, British command halted the attack on November 18th, finally ending the bloodshed on the Somme.

Nearly 5 months since the attack began, the Allied army had advanced a pathetic 6 miles and had not broken the German line. By the time the Battle of the Somme was over, more than 1 million men on each side had been killed or wounded. The British army received a baptism of fire with thousands of rat-infested corpses rotting away in shallow graves but still called the advance a strategic victory. Allied command would plan again for another attack. The Germans would build a brand-new line of defense, even more formidable, behind the Somme front. They conceded a small amount of territory but they would be more prepared to inflict more casualties on future advancing Allied soldiers.

Men have butchered each other during the war for ages, but modern warfare added a new dimension to the concept of blood-thirstiness. Souls found their way to heaven much quicker during the Great War. The two armies fought each other in one great suicide.

CHAPTER 1

THE HELL WHERE LAUGHTER GOES

It was late November 1916, at the Western Front. A German commander, Franz Fischer, climbed a worn wooden ladder to the top of the trench. He could feel the breeze stiffen as he gathered his coat around him. He gazed upon "no man's land." The mud-filled open space that divided the Deutsches Heer, also known as the Kaiser's men or the German army, from the Allied lines was littered with corpses of men and dead horses. Occasionally the wind would shift and the scent of rotting human and animal remains reeked in the air. Not today, the air was still and not a sound was heard. *When was the last time I witnessed a bird?* Franz wondered. Casting his gaze around the area, he caught a glimpse of a mutilated corpse stuck in the wire, the dead man's lipless mouth hanging open. *The poor bloke, his body must have been ripped to shreds from machine gunfire. At least he's in a better place now. A place where he can laugh and smile again.* A crow glided over to the corpse and began pecking on the corpse's face. It tore out an eye. Franz turned away from the site.

"No man's land" was a picture of hell on earth. Hell made worse if you stepped out there.

Suddenly artillery fire began to rain on the German position. It was time for hell again. Without delay, Franz bolted down the ladder and took cover against a wall of exposed earth. The trench buzzed with activity as men hurriedly took shelter against the walls or dove into fortified bunkers. Exploding shells continued to pepper relentlessly. He held his ears as he felt the vibrations of the pounding shells. With a look of surrender in his eyes, he resigned himself to remain still under the downpour that seemed to last forever.

The firing stopped abruptly. Immediately a shrill whistle blow sounded from the Allied line and was echoed back by others. The sound was replaced by a bugle call that typically signaled for an attack. The Allies would need to navigate huge craters caused by artillery, craters filled with muddy water and covering the area in a sporadic pattern. And they would have to traverse a complex network of barbed wire stained with blood. If they made it to the edge of the German line, another wall of barbed wire would be there to greet them, not to mention the machine guns.

With cries of "Huzzah!" a wave of British infantry charged out of their trenches as fast as their legs would take them. The Germans popped their heads up quickly and fired their rifles at the open targets that occasionally vanished in a crater. Once the advancing force encountered the first barbed wire, machine-gun fire opened up with deadly accuracy. Every line of fire for each gun had been clearly marked after countless uses. The advance slowed as the enemy came under punishing automatic fire. Countless men fell with a red spray on their uniforms. They crawled under the hail of bullets till they could see a few German "Stahlhelm" helmets then the force crept closer still. Finally, the British stopped returning fire, many dropped to one knee or took cover using the dead for shields. Unfortunately for them, the dug-in defenses were too formidable. It was carnage worthy of Dante's inferno. After the attacker's casualty rate piled up to nearly half dead or wounded, the order or cry of retreat sounded. A few lucky wounded were carried or dragged off during retreat; what remained were left behind to crawl back or perish. When the retreat was halfway back to their line, it was time for the Germans to counterattack.

Franz hollered, "Vorwärts für das Vaterland!" translated as "Forward for the Fatherland!" and slipped over the top of the trench. With bayonets fixed the Germans poured out from their trench in hot pursuit of the enemy. Those in retreat only stopped running when they dove back into their entrenched positions to return fire. This time it was the British machine guns that mowed down men like a sharp scythe to grass. The blood of young men soaked the earth as a sacrifice for their Fatherland. A few attackers came close enough to the defenses and managed to lob grenades into the crowded trenches. The resulting explosions were heard along with gurgling screams. That was as close as the counterattack came. It was impossible to take the unyielding British position with what was thrown against it. As was predictable whistles sounded, and it was the Germans' turn to run in retreat. And they did. Unlike the Germans, the British did not have to hold back machine gun fire to conserve ammunition. They had plenty of ammunition thanks to American generosity. The *ratatat* of machine-gun fire was relentless.

Franz fell back with his men. A dirty droplet of sweat rolled into his eye. While rubbing his eye, he was tripped by the body of a dead man sticking out of the mud. Franz's face planted into the wet muck. He staggered up and ran half-blinded by the mud on his face. Accepting an offer of an extended arm he made it back into the safety of the trench. The Allies and Germany continued to trade shots back and forth till eventually only a few scattered pops were heard. The whole engagement—attack and counter-attack— that took place lasted less than an hour before settling into silence. Only the heartbeats caused by the adrenaline rush still spoke in the silence.

Franz was one of the last to make it back. A leader in his mind was the first to jump into action and the last to leave it. Luck was on his side so far and he managed to survive another battle. He crouched so as not to show any visible target above the trench. Taking a deep, ragged breath, he patted his body slowly to feel for any injuries. After finding nothing but scratches and painful muscles that would lead to bruises later, he began to count his men. The casualty count resulted in 13 dead and 26 wounded from his company. He gave the numbers to the regimental command dispatchers sent to retrieve the numbers. Exhausted, he found a wooden crate to sit on for a moment to clear his head from the fog of battle. A fat rat scurried from underneath as he sat. He took off his helmet and placed it by his side. *I'm getting too old for this crap. Then again is anyone old enough to suffer through this?*

Franz was 32 but already streaks of grey interlaced his dark brown hair. Perhaps it was the hardships of war and responsibility for his men that gave him more grey. His face appeared to be cut from stone with dark brown eyes that held an endless pool so that you could barely see the pupils. Deep in those eyes lodged pearls of wisdom beyond his years.

Franz was a decorated officer who led an infantry company that was presented a mere skeleton of its effective strength. After the recent casualty count, it stood at 115 men. An infantry company typically consisted of a minimum of 150 men. He dug peat for a living prior to the war and also served in the army reserve. He did not enter the army as an officer. He worked his way up the ranks from Sergeant to Lieutenant via battle promotion. He was simply the only one qualified to take command after a poisonous mustard attack. The German-released mustard agent was doing well, destroying the enemy, until the wind shifted and brought the vapor to the attackers. Neary everyone was killed, including the prior company commander. The memory of that day forever etched his mind. The vivid images of bloodshot eyes, choking, and suffocating of his brothers in arms would follow him to his grave. Just the thought of it made him want to vomit, fall over, or both. In fighting this horrible war he had learned to be as hard as steel, but he thought he may shatter if he ever smelled the scent of mustard again.

A soldier he did not recognize stopped in front of him. The young man's uniform was remarkably clean. His face was disfigured with a prominent scar running across his face. An eye patch covered where one eye used to be. Franz stood up and subconsciously began to whack the dust from his dirty uniform.

"Lieutenant Fischer," the messenger said, "I have orders from the division command." The soldier handed a small envelope to Franz then quickly left.

Franz opened up the envelope. The order was short. A two-day leave would be granted for his company to spend at the rear and receive reinforcements. Franz grinned. It had been nearly two months since his company had been able to escape the battlefield.

Franz wasted no time. He gathered his two platoon Sergeants under his command and together they rounded up the men. Under full strength, his company should have had three platoons. Sergeant Hans Steuben led the first platoon. He was a simple farmer prior to the war and like Franz, he had earned a battle promotion. Hans worked his way up from private to sergeant by simply surviving. He was handsome. Although cut short, he had wavy blonde hair and blue eyes that a woman could get lost in. His bulk had slimmed some due to his diet at the front but he was still solid, both physically, and by temperament. Sergeant Adolf Gleue, who led the second platoon, was a mirror opposite. He held physical characteristics that only a mother would love. He appeared thin and gangly with large ears too big for his balding head. Although it looked like a strong wind could knock him down, what he lacked in physical strength he made up in spirit. He held a no surrender, no retreat attitude, along with a tongue like a wasp; Adolf was a force of his own.

The men in the company were instructed to gather what personal items they would need behind the line and quickly assemble in thirty minutes or lose their chance to go to the rear. The rear held rewards for the weary men, showers for their filth, hopes of better food, and an escape from their daily drudgery. The men rushed to assemble and soon they were headed out. In a time of peace, the trip would only be an hour but now it took several hours. They zig-zagged through, into, and out of the defensive works. The Germans attempted to avoid the high infantry losses of 1916 by withdrawing to new deeper and dispersed defenses. The deep defense was intended to negate the growing material strength of the Allies, particularly in artillery, and it succeeded in slowing the growth of Anglo-French battlefield success. The defenses were a fortress to overcome but a pain in the butt to get into and out of. Besides slippery mud, they had to manage not to trip on the wires—communication or barbed. Only the rats that scurried by their feet had no trouble navigating the labyrinth.

The company exited the defenses then reached open and dry space. The men began to relax their guard and take in the refreshing scenery. The grass fields and trees were a welcome sight from the imagery they were used to. Franz inhaled the smells of the air. The scent had an earthy smell just after rain. Through the trees, a small town could be seen at a distance.

Hans walked beside Franz. His eyes were blue ice beneath the helmet that encircled his brows. "It's nice that command has seen fit to bless us so. I look forward to a shower and I hope we're able to commandeer some good beer?"

Franz grinned. "Let's hope. I know my beer still surely misses me. She's a lady that has only seen the best. We used only water, hops, and malt as ingredients, keeping to the Reinheitsgebot standard of a good German beer. If the allies tasted it they would sue for peace for want of more."

Hans chuckled. "I'm sure you're right my friend. It's too bad we can't share it with them."

They arrived at the small town that appeared to be bursting at the seams. A once quiet farm town named Hurtgen, it was now under complete control by the German Army. Huge encampments were built for troops, horses, artillery, workshops, and dumps filled with equipment. In addition, reservoirs, pipelines, power stations, light railways, roads, and telephone networks were constructed. Besides hosting part of the German command, it held everything the front would need. Everything that was available, that is.

The men marched to the assembly area located at the division's recruit depot to pick up their replacements. The German war machine had no problem recruiting for the war effort. The German Constitution of April 16, 1871, stated every male was liable for military service, from his 17th to 45th birthday. It inspired mobilization by advertising everyone's duty within the war effort. The majority of individual soldiers believed that every order was sacred, and as a tiny low cog within the huge military machine, one had the duty to follow orders accordingly. Even if it meant charging machine gun fire needlessly to their deaths. The German Army worked hard to create "Esprit de Corps" within these Recruit Depots, thus creating a brotherly bond of local fellow countrymen, many of whom were family and friends. The depots traveled with their Division when moved. Unfortunately, it was not always possible to send the newly graduated recruits to companion regiments, so many of them became distributed throughout the army as they left the recruit depot wherever needed. In many ways, this practice reduced heavy losses for certain localities within Germany.

Twenty-four recruits were already in the assembly area waiting for them. Franz looked upon the new recruits. He never saw a German common soldier, however, employed, who did not seem to know exactly what he was doing and why he was doing it: The order came. Somebody else always had thought it out—that was that somebody's business, not his. The individual had been relieved of the function of thinking any thoughts upon the orders. The recruits looked between 17 and 18. The German nation needed replacements and overlooked many obstacles to service such as birthdates. They wore the uniform of soldiers but not in their hearts; they had yet to experience the trial of combat. They were boys. They held eyes eager to serve and destroy. Their bodies and uniforms were clean. Franz subconsciously glanced at his filthy uniform. He hadn't bathed in some time. Dirt was under his nails, dark like the peat he knew so well, and his clothes were caked with dried mud and dust all over them.

"*Beachtung!*" Franz hollered. The men snapped to attention. Franz licked his lips. "You men will be joining the First Company of the 25th Infantry Regiment, of First Army. Forget everything you have learned at the Recruiting Depot." The young men looked astonished. "You will be split into either the 1st or 2nd platoon. You will also be assigned a veteran. This veteran will be your battle buddy to show you the ropes. Listen closely to these men if you want to stay alive. This is all. Dismissed!"

The veterans and recruits intermingled. The recruits were jested, had their hair rubbed and backs slapped.

A veteran called out, "Well boys, your moms aren't here to wipe your noses nor your behinds."

Adolf added to the taunt. "Your rifle, your new mother, is a perfect woman. She's never moody, and she'll stay with you even if she is out of ammo."

Hans slapped Adolf on the shoulder. "Also she replaces your sweetheart. She'll always be there and never asks you for anything and doesn't mind if you go to sleep right after you use it."

The nervous recruits took the fun in stride and managed a few chuckles of their own. Although the veterans laughed it did not completely spread to their faces. It was as if they could not truly let go in the moment. They had witnessed hell that would forever subdue their laughter. There was something in the faces of those that saw the shadow of death first hand. The recruits noticed this and pondered when their faces would take on that same look.

After introductions, it was time for evening chow. The men quickly formed a line outside an open-air mess station. The food served was everything the men off the line dreamed of. They were given a piece of pork and beef bratwurst, boiled potato, a hunk of cheese and a large chunk of bread all served from a fat cook in his white heavily food-stained apron.

Adolf could not resist making fun of the cook's appearance. "How can anyone be that fat? I'm surprised there's any food left to serve us?"

The cook's face reddened briefly but it turned into a grin. "I do a lot of sampling to make sure it's worthy of you, my lord."

The men laughed.

Franz waited till everyone was served. A good officer always eats last. After his plate was filled he gave his sausage to Hans. The big man could always use more food. Hans was not complaining. "You don't want your sausage? Oh, that's right you're. . . . I forget."

Franz gave him an annoyed look. "Did you mean you forgot I was a Jew?" Franz feigned anger.

"Yup, that's it. Pigs are quite disgusting. I'll give you that." Hans snickered. "But they sure taste good."

Franz winked. "I wouldn't know, but you're welcome."

"Oh. Thanks."

Franz cleared his throat. One eyebrow rose.

"Sir."

"Tell me, Sergeant, what do you think of the new men?"

"Men? They're more like green potatoes just taken from the ground too early, but they're still potatoes and we will need to make use of them."

"Good because you have no choice. I assigned them each a veteran so they don't get into too much trouble. The usual trend is to not give them the time of day because they haven't paid their dues or not to get too attached to someone that may not live longer than a scoop of coal on a cold day. That crap ends with this company. The veterans will teach or I'll teach them something to remember."

"I read you, sir."

After eating, the company moved into the newly constructed barracks in town. For the veterans, it was like having rooms in a fancy hotel compared to where they lived recently. They washed away the dirt of the battlefield and changed into fresh uniforms. Some men went out immediately to enjoy entertainment in town but most relaxed on their bunks waiting for the mail to be delivered.

Time always seems to slow down in military life. Every soldier regardless of how long they've served suffers from a version of home-sickness. Occasionally the recurrent theme of postcards and letters dispatched to the front lines was temporarily eased by the arrival of a parcel from home. The distribution of these packages was an enormous enterprise that sometimes threatened the efficient functioning of every nation's military postal system. Families were asked to keep their shipments to a minimum and were reminded that military regulations prohibited the shipment of liquids, food, and perishable items. Few regulations were more consistently ignored for the duration of the war.

The post-delivery came with letters and plenty of the coveted parcels. Out came every manner of sweets, chocolate, biscuits, and candies from the packages. The men traded and swapped goodies from home. Franz received a box of Turkish delights. After tossing a few in his pocket, he shared with his men. Hans handed him a large piece of his grandmother's gingerbread. Fair payment for the sausage given to him earlier.

Shortly after the mail arrived a delivery of beer came in. The men were served beer regularly, even at the front, but rarely in a decent amount. The German Government, recognizing the value of beer, issued it as a ration to the German Army and had requisitioned 20 percent of the entire output of all breweries for this purpose. Beer, besides being palatable and refreshing for the men, was appreciated for its health properties. It was frequently prescribed by physicians to repair the waste of tissue, conserve strength, and aid the assimilative and digestive processes. Franz could care less about the health benefits for the men; it was a way for them to escape their reality for a time and forget their troubles. The grim reaper could take them at any time on the battlefield, but not tonight. Tonight they would cast their worries on barrels of beer.

CHAPTER 2

HOME IS WHERE THE HEART LIVES

Franz's dreams took him back to his modest home located in the province of Westphalia within the Kingdom of Prussia, part of the German Empire. It was late in the evening after another day of hard labor, he sat relaxed on his favorite chair in his living room. The well-worn chair was dark stained, made from walnut wood carefully taken care of since it was handed down through his family, the Fisher's, for generations. Despite the darkness outside, the room was well lit from a combination of oil lamps, candles, and a roaring fireplace. He watched as flames in the fireplace curled and swayed, flicked this way and that, crackled as the dry wood burned. His mind escaped to the tranquility of the moment. He lit his polished wood pipe and puffed out cloud circles in the air. A movement by his feet. He felt his old German Shepherd named Schwartz curled up beside his feet.

Erna, his wife, walked in and using her fingertips gently caressed his neck, then she sat on her wooden chair beside him. A beauty in Franz's eyes. He loved her curves of softness that made those portrait models look as paper-thin as they are. She was robust and real. A sunflower that made Franz bloom every time he thought of her.

Franz's three daughters walked in the room together, laughing and giggling. They all had their mother's dark brown eyes and sense of humor. Herta, age 16 with long dark brown hair tied with a blue ribbon, appeared more robust than her mother. She was a born thinker that always asked why. Anne, age 12 with light brown hair, was as robust as her mother. She was always optimistic, never seeing a glass half empty. Emma, age 10, was thin with her curly hair the same color as her mother's, dirty blonde. She had the face of her mother with a perpetual hint of mischief in her eyes. It is difficult for any parent to have favorites among their children, but to Franz, Emma came close. She radiated joy in any situation. Just being in her presence made Fanz smile.

Herta held her cello and looked up at her father with a glow in her eyes that beckoned permission to play. Franx returned the look with a nod up and down. The graceful instrument rested between her knees, her arm held the bow just above the four strings spanning the length of the cello. The mahogany wood instrument curved inwards at the sides, much like womanly curves, right down to the endpin which touched the floor. When she finally allowed herself the pleasure of dragging the bow across the C string, a deep resounding hum filled the room. The music of Bach's Cello Suite No 1 played full and satisfyingly. She continued the song, her left-hand fingers dancing at the top, while her right hand moved back and forth, both working together to create a sound that paralleled even the most heavenly voice.

The two youngest girls, Anne and Emma, giggled as they danced around the room with each other pretending they were at a ball. His wife filled the room with warm laughter as she watched their fun. Schwartz stretched out, stood up, and barked at the two. This made his wife only laugh harder. Listening to the music and laughter in the room was a symphony of pleasure to Franz's ears. He lost himself in the moment watching his loved ones enjoy themselves. The living room captured happiness unbounded.

The sound of bugles, playing morning reveille, woke Franz to reality. He stirred slowly, his head pounded from last night's drinking debauchery. With a great effort, he forced himself not to rub his temples. He went to the bathroom sink and splashed ice cold water on his face, which washed the crusties out of the corner of his eyes, but did nothing for his bloodshot eyes. *Coffee!* He needed a strong brew to wake him and clear the fog from his head. He moved quickly. After hastily dressing and grabbing his rifle, he moved with purpose outside the building to the call of a strong brew or a cup of Joe as the Americans would call it. He knew the American Navy now prohibited alcohol aboard ships and that disgruntled sailors had started calling coffee a "cup of Joe" out of bitterness.

The coffee was already prepared in the mess area. Franz poured a cup the way he loved it. Black as coal. He took a gulp. Pain! The coffee scorched his mouth and burned his tongue. He took a seat on one of the many scattered wooden stools then blew on his coffee. This time he took a small sip. *One more day and we will be headed back to the front. What the men need is an escape. A moment of peace before they return to perdition. To see a little of what they are fighting for.* His mind brought him to one of the few places he knew he could find peace. He was up early enough and had no excuses. The Saturday Shabbat morning service called to him.

The Jews were fortunate to have the favor and protection of the Kaiser. Over 100,000 Jews joined the German Army to serve the German Empire. The war ministry approved the service of 8 rabbis, 6 served on the western front and 2 served in the East. Their function included burial services, hospital visits, distributing religious literature, and much more. Although they were allowed to join the German war machine, access to higher ranks was rare. Franz's promotion to an officer in the army was rare. Many that coveted promotion converted to Christianity. The Jews in the

Ottoman Empire and the Russian military were not treated with such freedom. Their roles were restricted to non-combat and to serve their nation they had to join a labor unit.

Franz went to services at a field tent turned into a temporary synagogue. A small wooden foldable table served as an altar dressed in white cloth for the rabbi to do his Torah reading. The rabbi appeared wearing a black coat that covered over his grey uniform. He wore a black hat, round with a large brim. A heavy gold chain with David's shield and the two tablets of the covenant adored his neck. He spoke a quick prayer before he wrapped himself in a wool prayer shawl, also called a tallit.

Baruch atah adonai	Blessed are you, Lord our God,
Eloheinu melech ha olam	Ruler of the Universe,
Asher kidishanu b'mitzvotav	Who has sanctified us with your mitzvot,
Vitzivanu l'hitatef b'tzitzit.	And commanded us to wrap ourselves in tzitzit.

The rabbi proceeded to read from the Torah. In a final prayer, he said, "We stand before our God: Our strength is in Him. In Him are the truth and the dignity of our history. In Him is the source of our survival through every change, our firm stance in all our trials. Our history is the history of spiritual greatness, spiritual dignity. We turn to it when attack and insult are directed against us, when need and suffering press in upon us. The Lord led our fathers from generation to generation. He will continue to lead us and our children through our days.

"We stand before our God; we draw strength from His Commandments, which we obey. We bow down before Him, and we stand upright before men. It is Him we serve and in Him remain steadfast in all the changes around us. We put our faith in Him in humility and our way ahead is clear, we see our future.

"The whole House of Israel stands before its God at this hour. Our prayer, our faith, and our belief are that of all the Jews on earth. We look upon each other and know ourselves, we raise our eyes to the Lord and know what is eternal.

"Behold, He that guardeth Israel shall neither slumber nor sleep.

"He who maketh peace in His high places, may He make peace for us and for all Israel and say ye, Amen.

"We are filled with sorrow and pain. In silence, we will give expression to all that which is in our hearts, in moments of silence before our God. This silent worship will be more emphatic than any words could be."

After service ended the soldiers gathered to enjoy fellowship. The rabbi walked around giving out medallions made of thin metal with the star of David stamped on it. Franz found himself shaking hands then talking with Otto Frank who served with the Lichtmesstrupp, a unit that analyzed where enemy artillery fire came from. Otto lived by the Rhine River. He would describe himself as a liberal Jew that valued the traditions and holidays but did not strictly observe all religious laws.

Otto spoke in a cheerful tone, "My Eema is so persistent her son will get married that's all she writes about. Doesn't she realize there's a war going on?" Otto continued in a more subdued voice, "It would be nice to have a family of my own one day. Make good memories to replace what we've seen."

"Although it has its challenges, a family is a blessing," Franz said. "Many people are lost in their quest for happiness. I tell you the truth, the search does not have to be so difficult. Seek the love of family and you will find it. I am blessed to have my wife Erna and three daughters, Herta, Emma, and Anne."

Otto sheepishly smiled. "I like the name Anne. Anne Frank has a pleasant ring to it. If I ever survive this war and have a child, I may use it."

"Feel free my friend. First, you will need to find a wife."

The rabbi approached them. "Did I hear someone mention finding a wife? I once asked a couple in my synagogue back home, who had been married over 50 years, what was the secret to their long marriage. They answered that the wife made all the small decisions and he, the big ones. The small decisions like where to live, which house to buy, which synagogue to attend. I asked the husband what were the big decisions in life that he chose for the family. He turned to his wife and told me the only big decision he ever made was to marry his wife."

Franz and Otto looked at each other than at the rabbi. Laughter filled the air. For a moment the men forget the battlefield. Soon they would return to the hell where men and laughter go.

CHAPTER 3

AMERICA'S FAVORITE PASTIME

It was April 5, 1917; the new warmth of spring had arrived. The trees were sprouting new buds. They had shed their winter covers, the layers they sheltered within, and now boldly sought the sun, renewed in her brilliance. The smell of fresh-cut grass lingered in the air. Perhaps the biggest evidence of spring's return was America's favorite pastime. Baseball.

Two bitter rivals were facing off on a baseball field. Hope High School located on the east side of the City of Providence, Rhode Island, was tied 3-3 against their opponent from Burrillville High School, located in Harrisville, Rhode Island, at the top of the ninth with one out. The umpires chosen from the crowd before the first pitch were standing alert. This year teams used a first base umpire as a recently added position, an improvement from the prior one umpire system.

The home crowd booed as Myles Archambault approached the plate. Myles gave a few practice swings then stepped into the batter's box staring down the pitcher. He was a short boy 5'4, but what he lacked in size he made up for in muscle. He shook his head lightly to move the long brown curls from his eyes. His deep brown eyes, as rich as the earth's soil, asked the pitcher to bring it. The pitcher threw a fastball. Crack, the ball flew from the bat. Myles sprinted down the first baseline. The ball bounced off the ground and quickly into the glove of the shortstop. The shortstop threw the ball to first base. It was going to be close. "Safe!" yelled the first base umpire as Myles's foot touched the base a hair before the ball reached the first baseman's glove. Myles patted the dirt off his uniform and prepared mentally to steal second base. The next batter came up to the plate. Myles let out a long breath then moved off the base slightly prepared to dive back to first base if he needed to. "Strike one!" yelled the home plate umpire with a raised right hand. Myles inched a little closer to second base. The pitcher suddenly threw the ball to first base. Myles dove. "Safe!" cried the first base umpire. Myles dusted himself off and moved closer to second base again. "Strike two!" yelled the home plate umpire.

Myles's heart raced as he scanned the freshly green painted wood scoreboard. With the game tied in the last inning with only two outs remaining his team needed a run. With the smack of a bat, the hitter made contact with the ball. The ball soared into the air and was caught easily by the outfielder. Myles barely made it back to first base after running on the hit. A bead of sweat rolled down his face and his stomach knotted up. *Only one more out and the game is over. Come on, Al, you can do it.*

Albert Paolino came out of the dugout. Al was a chunky kid known for his heart of gold. Jeers erupted from the opposing teams as Al locked eyes with the pitcher. They were, after all, playing at Burrillville's home field. "Strike one!" yelled the home plate umpire. Another pitch and: "Strike two!" Then Al made solid contact, a line drive to left field. Myles bolted safely to second base.

Now he was on second, Al on first, and George Milton, the team's best hitter, coming to the plate. Myles called out, "Come on, George!"

George was not only the team's best hitter but according to girls also the best-looking player on the team. He was a stocky boy with wavy blond locks of hair and blue eyes. He took a few practice swings then made his way to the plate. It was time to make it or break it. George called for time. Myles wiped the sweat from his brow. He clenched his fists by his side with his heart pounding about to explode. The pitcher threw the first pitch. "Strike one!" roared the home plate umpire. Then: "Strike two!" Then the most magnificent sound to Myles's ears as the bat struck the ball, a line drive to center, right over Myles's head. Myles took off running with all his might, rounding third base as the centerfielder ran to the ball, picked it up, and fired it toward home. Now it was a race between Myles and the flying ball. Myles dove headfirst with abandon, his palm brushing across the plate just as the catcher caught it and applied the tag. "Safe!" the Umpire yelled. While Providence fans cheered, Myles dusted himself off and made his way to the dugout. The next batter came to the plate then struck out.

Providence High took the field. Myles took his position in left field, watching the action closely. Their pitcher was on fire, striking out the first two batters with ease. No contact was made with the ball. The last batter made contact but every hit was fouled until a high pop-up was snatched out of the air by the catcher. *We won!* A pandemonium of whoops and shouts erupted from the winning team's fans. The opposing crowd sat in silence. Myles and his teammates flew to the center of the field cheering and shaking hands. Myles was crushed in a wave of players. Crushed with a victory. Myles hollered, "We're number one!" till his voice failed him.

No celebration lasts forever but it can forever burn in our memories. Time passed and the celebration came to an end. The spectators began to depart. Myles spotted Kathy Miller, his girlfriend, waiting patiently for him near the players' dugout. She wore a plain white puffed blouse and a fluted earthen-colored skirt with a blue ribbon. She had straight long brown hair and a beaky nose like a cartoon character. He made his way to her and they embraced. Kathy was not the most beautiful girl in school but to Myles, she was his princess. It was her passion for life that gave her beauty. She peered over her spectacles, tilting her head forward just enough to see that behind those lenses were eyes of blue, filled with infinite curiosity. "You won the whole nine yards baby."

Myles did not say anything, just held her like a grizzly bear. He then gave her a quick peck on the lips. He did not want to be overzealous, her father could be near.

"We sure gave those Burrillville bumpkins something to remember us by. They'll talk less smack now!"

Myles was nudged from behind. His head spun and he released his embrace. "You coming, Myles, the train's about to leave the station, you dingbat," grinned George. "And I don't want to lose my ride."

Myles turned to Kathy with a slight frown. "Tootles, Kathy, I'll see you when I get home."

Kathy's voice took on mock sternness. "You will if you know what's good for you." A quick embrace then Myles followed George to the parents' parade of Ford Model T's that would take the boys home. The characteristic loud chirping and clanking of engines were heard from the T's with an occasional horn sound. Myles searched for a familiar vehicle. *There it is.* His father, Frank Archambault, sat in his four-door car waiting. Myles popped open the squeaky front passenger side door. "Hey, Dad, can we give George a lift?"

Frank turned to George. "Hey, George. Sure, hop in, We're not headed out just yet boys. Let's wait a little bit and make sure no one else needs a ride."

They waited with only the sounds of T's to entertain them. Myles wished one day they'd put a music box in a car. Frank cleared his throat. "Sorry I couldn't catch the game, son." A slight sigh. "I know it means a lot to you. I heard you boys clobbered Burrillville. Good for you. When I played for Hope High we didn't do so well."

"I know, dad. You see most of my games though."

"Having a car does help."

"You're a boss, if you gotta work, you gotta work. Maybe one day you'll own the textile mill."

Frank puffed out his chest in exaggeration. "Wouldn't that be nice?" He rustled Myles' hair.

With no players needing a ride, Myles and Frank delivered George to his family then went home. The Model T's knocking engine shut off and continued to rattle for a few seconds.

"Look at little miss impatient." Frank pointed to the front entrance of the house.

Myles' kid sister Lillian, known as Lilly, stood with arms crossed in front of her. Shilo, the family dog, a Staffordshire terrier mix, stood by her side. She was wearing her favorite plaid dress with a tied red ribbon with a bow to her left side. She was as thin as a twig with two long brown ponytails, one to the left and one to the right. She allowed the men inside the door but then blocked any further movement with her body. Her eyes were squinted and her arms remained crossed. With the eyes of a tigress, she locked them with Myles.

Lilly exploded in words, "So did you win?"

"Of course, sis, we clobbered 'em."

Lilly smiled. "I would have loved to have seen that. Mom thinks I see too many. She made me stay home to help her fix dinner. It turns out it will be a victory feast."

Myles bent down to pet Shilo.

Well, how did you do?" Said Lilly.

"I scored the winning run after George saved the day with his swing."

"Oh, the silent movie star-looking one. He's so dreamy."

"Oh, Lilly, you're hopeless. Let us pass, we're dang hungry."

Mother appeared. "Lilly let them pass. I don't want their food to get cold. And this time, Lilly, no scraps for Shilo at the table."

Lilly gave Shilo a guilty look. "Yes, mom."

Lilly put her arms down and let the men escape past her.

"Thank you for your protection." Frank winked at Mary

Mary smiled. "Now the both of you get yourself washed up and to the table. Chop, chop."

The men sped away to change to wash and change to fresh clothes. They returned to sit at the dinner table already set with food. Mary and Lilly were already seated. The aroma of Mary's cooking made their stomachs growl. Plates were full of potato hash and a heaping scoop of clam chowder over the top with a side of baked beans. It was Lilly's turn to say grace. She crossed her fingers in prayer. "Dear Lord, thank you for the food we are about to eat. Thank you for the victory over Burrillville. They're such Schlocks."

Mother gave Lilly dagger eyes. "Lilly?"

Lilly lowered her head. She spoke quickly, "Thank you, Jesus, Amen."

After dinner, it was time for an Archambault family tradition. They couldn't remember when it started but it was part of being an Archambault to engage in a family discussion. If they were short of topics, they would discuss headlines in the paper. Recent headlines were all about President Wilson, who originally pledged to remain neutral in the conflict with Europe but was now asking Congress to declare war. On April 4, the Senate voted 82 to 6 to declare war; the public waited in anticipation for the vote from the House. Wilson said the declaration was "To keep the world safe for democracy," but the flashpoint was America's rage over the "Zimmerman Telegram." The British had intercepted and given to President Wilson a secret telegram urging the Mexicans, America's southern neighbor, to enter into hostilities with the U. S. in return for (Germany promised) the restoration of the territory Mexico lost in the Mexican-American War, including New Mexico, Arizona, and Texas.

Frank tossed the daily newspaper on the table. "So do you think we are justified to go to war with the Hun?"

Myles turned. "I'd say the Germans using those sneaky U-boats is enough to declare war. They sank the Lusitania, nearly 2,000 killed, more than 120 U.S. citizens and we didn't even retaliate. We should have declared war then. You can only poke an animal for so long, at some point, it will turn and bite you."

"I'd say that war doesn't solve anything," said Mary.

Frank raised an eyebrow. "I disagree. Don't get me wrong, people suffer in war but it does solve problems. Heck, this country wouldn't be here if not for war. Does anyone remember a little war called the American Revolution?"

"Here, here dad." Myles piped in.

"I'm with mom." Lilly declared.

"You would be," Myles harrumphed.

Lilly smiled. "Well, someone has to keep the boys in check."

When dinner was finished, Lilly cleared off the table with Shilo in tow. Shilo helped her with the cleaning. He wasn't fed from the table but he was able to lick the plates clean before Lilly washed them.

Frank grinned at Myles. "Care to play some chess before bed?"

"Sure, one game. I swear you cheat."

"Hah, no cheating, just a lot of experience. I chose the chess team versus the baseball team in high school. I tell you the truth, you're getting better. What is the score? Not that I keep counting."

"At least thirty to zip."

Frank won in only twelve moves and Myles went up to his room. With a yawn, he stretched out on his bed. He went over today's game in his mind. Myles knew he would never be able to play professional baseball but he loved the game. Just for those two or three hours, there was really no place he would rather be. Thoughts trickled in about his future after high school. He would be graduating soon and he didn't have much of a plan. He had no idea what he wanted to do for work, the thought of joining his father at his mill was not appealing. Thoughts drifted to the family discussion at the dinner table. *If it comes to war. The Hun ain't going to win any game against us. It's a stalemate over there. With our help, the British and French will get a pinch-hit to help get 'em the win. I'd be a dewdropper if the call came and I didn't serve.* Eventually, fatigue from the game set in and his eyes closed.

The following morning, April 6, the *Providence Journal* reported the news. The House of Representatives voted 373 to 50 in favor of adopting a war resolution against Germany. It was only the fourth time Congress had declared war; the others were the War of 1812, the War with Mexico in 1846, and the Spanish-American War of 1898. There was a problem. Although the newspapers screamed war, the country and army were inadequate at best. The current standing army, including the National Guard of 300,000, would need to grow to a million-man army quickly. Fortunately, there was an American spirit. Like a sleeping Giant once woken, there was no stopping it.

CHAPTER 4

SHOULD I STAY OR SHOULD I GO

The end of school for Myles always led to summer vacation. This summer would be his last vacation before entering the real world. The world where childhood ends and adult life begins. While Myles pondered his future, he continued his usual end-of-school-year routine for the last time. Most of his summers were spent with his grandfather Everett in his garden located within Warren, Rhode Island. Myles would help with whatever grandfather needed. What Everett didn't need for himself he would sell at a farm stand in front of his house. Myles received 25% of the profits as payment for his efforts. Myles enjoyed the money earned but he enjoyed the company of his grandfather more. Everett worked right beside him humming and whistling and telling imaginative stories. What Myles appreciated the most was his grandfather's gift for listening. Myles could discuss everything or anything. Everett would nod and comment but he would never interrupt till you were finished. His grandfather had a gift.

A wrinkled sun-tanned face peered out from under a brim straw hat, which was the only thing covering his bald head unless it was fringes of grey. Everett patted the sweat from his brow with an old dirty red handkerchief. "The sun kicked my butt today. Let's call it a day. There'll be plenty of work left for us tomorrow. Those tomato plants ain't gonna plant themselves."

They walked into the house then Everett poured two tall glasses of water from a white porcelain pitcher on the kitchen table. "I see you were lagging today. Your mind looks occupied," Everett said. He motioned for Myles to take one of the chairs around the kitchen table. Myles and Everett sat. Everett raised an eyebrow. "Tell me what's bugging you?"

There were two main thoughts that troubled Myles. Myles was considering joining the army and proposing to his girlfriend Kathy. Myles took a gulp of water while collecting his thoughts.

His grandfather had never served in the service nor sacrificed for his country, but he loved his nation. Everett's father fought in the American Civil war, but after his experience in the brutal war became a pacifist. He forbade any of his sons to enlist. Myles never met his great grandfather but he heard some grizzly battle stories his grandfather did share. Probably exaggerated a bit to scare his sons from ever joining the army.

In a large gulp, Myles finished his water. "Grandfather, I'm thinking of enlisting in the army. We are at war with the Hun. It is my duty to serve. How can I call myself an American if I don't defend my country?"

"You don't need to convince me. It's not my decision, it's yours. I will support whatever decision you make. I will not tell you what to do. You need to decide for yourself. I will tell you, though, to follow your heart. If it's beating to go, do it. If it doesn't beat for it, do not go. If you don't follow your heart, you may live to regret it."

"I have. I'm going to do it," said Myles, his voice filled with conviction.

Everett grinned, "I wish I'd had the nerve to stand up to my father. I feel that it is important to serve your country. To sacrifice for what you think is right. It is better to live life and do what you think is right, as long as you keep the good Lord's will in mind with your decisions. Your father did not serve because of my influence, I think it's time to break the chain in the family. I'm sure you will make us proud."

Myles thought his next question about his possible proposal to Kathy could be a sensitive subject. His Grandma Rose had passed away a long time ago. He had never met her. She had suffered from mental illness all her life, according to Everett, which was made worse after the birth of her only child Frank, but she refused to seek treatment. It was postpartum depression but they did not know it at the time. She and Everett got into a heated argument one night. She walked out on him. That night she waded off into the Kickamuit River. It was winter. When she finally snapped out of whatever spell captured her, she waded back to shore. What the water didn't kill pneumonia did and she died a miserable death. His grandfather never remarried and raised his son alone.

"Grandpa, what do you think about Kathy?"

"Are you thinking of wedding her?"

"I can't get anything past you."

"This decision I will give you my grandfatherly advice, like it or not. Believe me, there's a lot of fish in a vast ocean. You need to make sure to choose the right one. It's not like in my day. We had fewer options. Today you can court and romance a girl and get to know her before you decide. If it's not the right one, you can make up your mind at any time to end the relationship, for any reason, and go to court another." He patted Myles on the shoulder. "Once you marry, it's forever; it's a covenant with her and the Almighty. Through sickness and health, there is no escape. A woman's values and brain will make her a good wife and a good parent, not her looks. Also, sorry to burst your bubble, but it's not about love. A person's love is fragile and it won't help with the daily chores. Promise me you will not marry her before you ship out. Don't go the way of those idiots rushing into marriage before they ship out. A choice that is taken in ignorance often leads to disaster. Away, you will have time to reflect on her. You will have plenty of time to decide if she is the one. If it's meant to be it will be."

Everett held out his hand. Myles shook it.

"Ok." Myles nodded. "I promise, but it's gonna cost you some of your summer brew. Let's share a mug of your finest."

Everett left the kitchen and returned with 2 amber-filled stoneware pottery brown glazed mugs. Myles sipped off the top foam. It went down smoothly. "Grandfather, you get better and better with every batch."

"You think so? Maybe we should go into business together." Everett chuckled. "We'd probably make more money than vegetables at the farm stand." He pulled out a deck of cards and a tin can filled with buttons. Let's play a few rounds of Faro before bed. And Myles, after your evening prayers, don't get caught up thinking so deeply as you do. What you need is a good night's sleep. You'll have your decision when you wake up in the morning about the army. Cheers."

They clicked mugs.

After a few refills of beer, they played cards late into the evening. Myles made his way to bed. Although he would go with whatever his gut said first thing in the morning, it didn't prevent his mind from overthinking. He tossed and turned throughout the night.

He dreamed his assigned army unit had just arrived at the front. The enemy defenses were about one hundred feet away. The air was thick. Thick with black smoke over the battlefield. His unit stood waiting for the signal to climb out and charge. He noticed a few German helmets sticking out. He took aim. Click. No bullets. *Weird.*

"Charge!" yelled an officer nearby. The Americans poured out of the trench. Remarkably, the Germans also charged at the same time. The forces slid to a halt a moment before impact. They began to shake each other's hands and give each other back slaps. A fiddle was produced and music began to play. The men made fools of themselves as they danced. The Germans brought out beer jugs from ammo crates. It was a circus. An American officer called the men to gather around him.

"The war has ended but the world will forever remember your sacrifice and courage. We have witnessed the last war between nations. What you have done here will echo in eternity."

Huh, I didn't even fire a shot.

When Myles woke he had his answer.

CHAPTER 5

GOODBYE

In New England, the weather is known for being inconsistent. To turn on a dime. Cold one day then hot another day. The weather today was unexpectedly warm. The sky was cloudless and the sun's warmth kissed Myles and Kathy as they walked on Blackstone Boulevard parallel to the trolley line located at the east side of Providence, Rhode Island. A sporadic light breeze disturbed the lush green foliage and trees that gave some shade but both offered little relief from the mugginess. Myles regretted his choice of clothing and wished he chose cooler clothes. He was dressed in grey wool pants, a white long-sleeve cotton shirt, and a sporty wool newsboy cap. His shirt was already starting to stick to him. Kathy somehow appeared immune to the weather. She wore an Asher navy blue dress worn almost to the ground.

Myles had known Kathy since elementary school. As a child, he used to tease and pick on her. When Kathy began to grow up and fill out, she caught his attention. They were officially dating. Dating was a new term that replaced "calling" as a favored model of Romance. In 1914, *The Ladies' Home Journal*, an authority on American propriety, printed an issue supporting dating, previously mistrusted by parents, ushering in a new era. Both sets of parents allowed dating but they needed to know where the couple was at all times. If anything improper happened, that would be the end of the sweethearts.

Kathy was all giggles today. There was nothing that could warm Myles's heart more than seeing her amazing smile. The beauty of her smiles would usually help him forget whatever troubles worried him. Today they did very little. He was concerned about how Kathy would react to his decision to enlist in the army. He liked to believe he could make her smile. Today he hoped he did not make her cry. Myles wanted to keep her smiling a little longer. He turned to Kathy. Her large blue eyes held a playful glint. Myles said, "Hey, I got one for yah. A foolish fellow with money was asked how he funded his travel abroad, and he replied 'by my wits, of course.' The other retorted, 'You must have traveled very cheaply then.'"

Kathy looked puzzled for a second. She did not roar with laughter but Myles received a cracked smile for his effort. Kathy's hand brushed his hand, sending him goosebumps.

"Very funny," she said sarcastically.

"Want to hear another one?" Myles implored.

He wiped the perspiration off his forehead with his sleeve. "I have one about a grandpa and his young grandson at a restaurant?"

Kathy sighed softly, "You know I think maybe we should just enjoy the walk together. I can not stay long. I promised my mum I'd go wild berry picking with her."

They continued to walk side by side. A few people passed by but did not disturb the couple. It was as if only the two existed. A fresh breeze stirred up strongly. Myles inhaled deeply, capturing a whiff of the sweet scent of nearby flora. He needed to tell Kathy about his decision to join the army. A decision that could forever alter his life or lose it. Soon his life would change, but he refused to let go of the here and now. He embraced this moment, carving it into his memory. Myles suddenly let out a loud sneeze.

Kathy retorted, "God bless you, or *Gott schütze dich* as my Opa says. Did I tell you my Opa still can't believe we are going to war with Germany? He is adamant we stay out of it. He says it's Europe's problem. Let them deal with it. He left Europe years ago to escape their problems. I agree with him. Let Europe continue their foolishness. Keep us out of it."

Myles gulped. It was now or never to tell her. Myles's heart pounded in his chest. *Well, best to get it over with. How can I go off to war if I'm afraid to talk to my own girlfriend?* He held Kathy's hand.

He croaked, "I'm going to enlist in the army, Kathy. I wanted you to hear it first before I tell anyone. My mother and father will not approve but many of my friends already enlisted, those old enough to sign up. Why wait to be drafted? I'll be 18 in August. I can sign up without their consent if necessary."

Myles looked at Kathy, waiting for her reaction. Kathy looked frazzled. She closed her eyes then tears burst forth. She had read about the horrors and suffering at the battlefield from newspapers and teachers had described the war in detail in school. At the moment she could only imagine the worst for Myles. Her tears ran like water from a dam bursting down her face. She shook and trembled. Myles pulled her to his chest and held her close. He waited until the sobs subsided. He gathered both her hands into his and looked into Kathy's eyes. "I promise that I will return to you. Come hell or high water."

She looked directly at Myles. Her beautiful dark blue eyes were now swollen and puffy. "How could you do this to me? You're so young," she sputtered. "You should wait to join."

His lips brushed her ear as he spoke softly. "Wait till what, Kathy? I do not want to miss the war. I have dreamed of serving my country. It's not right for others to go off while others stay home. I've made up my mind, Kathy. I will not turn back from my decision." He stared intently into her eyes. "I'm sorry."

A clinking of bells. A streetcar moved toward them slowly down the trolley line. Myles and Kathy moved away from the steel rails.

They watched the trolley pass, its trolley pole skidding along the overhead electrified wire. The driver chimed the bell and waved at them. They returned the wave. The sound of the screeching car faded as it rambled on.

Kathy's fingers tightened on his arm. Her nails sunk in uncomfortably. Her voice was serious. "I will hold you to your promise. You better return to me."

Kathy shook a little, afraid that moving would cause more tears to flow. Her smile was definitely gone. They finished the walk in silence. The silence caressed his heart, doing little to ease his mind. But it did a little. Myles walked slowly, feeling relieved. He had told Kathy he would join the army. His next step was to do it.

CHAPTER 6

MECHANICAL MONSTER

It was early morning over the German defensive positions. Guards stood vigilant, watching over No Man's Land. The majority of the army was tucked deep under the earth. Like ants, they nested in chambers and corridors, waiting for orders to swarm.

The glow from a small iron stove cast a dim light on the room. Only the dark silhouette of double-stacked bunks could be seen. "Ah- Ah- Achoo," Franz sneezed.

"*Gesundheit*! whispered Hans across from him. Hans had been snoring just a little while ago. Franz hoped he wasn't the cause of waking him. Franz sat up on his bunk. He was battling a cold. He felt like a train had run over him, leaving his body crushed. His bones shivered despite his thick blanket. The stove in his sleeping area barely seemed to give off any heat to fight the chills. At least they had a stove. He was grateful for the sleeping area that was dug nearly forty feet deep for safety. Besides protection from the enemy artillery, it offered the comfort of metal bunks, a stove, and electric lights. It was not home but it was paradise compared to the alternative of living full time in a miserable trench.

Franz reached out and grabbed his canteen from his belt hanging on his bunk post. He swallowed a large mouthful of water. This simple act of swallowing cool water meant to soothe only burned on the way down. He slowly moved off his bunk and blew his nose on a dirty rag. He wished he could clear the fog in his head as he blew. His body ached from head to toe and he felt as weak as a newborn lamb. He knew his body needed rest but his mind had a worse enemy and it was called boredom. His spirit needed to work more than his body needed to heal. Plenty of time for rest in the grave.

Sniffling, he got dressed into his uniform, put on his helmet then grabbed his rifle. The dirty rag he held was placed in his coat pocket for future use.

Hans called from across the room as Franz walked towards the entrance. "You sound like a congested pig. Why don't you let me take sentry duty for you?"

Franz pulled out his rag from his pocket then blew his nose. "I'm fine. The air will do me good."

"If you say so, you're the boss. Here take a swig of this."

Franz walked over to take a bottle of brandy from Han's outstretched arm.

"Good spirits from home," said Hans.

Franz took a swallow and immediately began a hacking cough.

"Easy there, just a thimbleful is fine. It ain't much but it will give you some comfort from the cold."

Franz returned the bottle then departed. A breeze gusted through the trench and threatened to freeze the mud caking to his clothing. He shivered as his body adjusted to the cold.

Every man in his company, including himself, shared all the duties. As a company commander, he easily could have avoided every work detail but he believed it was important to set an example for his men. A good commander is the first to charge and lead from the front, Franz always thought.

As he made his way to the guard post the stench of decay traveled with him and he hoped that what squished under his boots was mud even though his boot heel held a bloodstain. *Dang rats!*

Franz recognized the thin nineteen-year-old boy with a crooked nose and large ears. His eyes looked glazed as he handed Franz a looking glass and thick wool blanket.

Franz drew a ragged breath. "See anything out there, Private Richthofen?

Richthofen looked up in thought.

Franz frowned. "You didn't catch any z's did you?"

"No sir. I got sleepy once and poured my canteen over my head. That did the trick, let me tell you. I thought my eyes would freeze shut. Brrrr. I haven't seen any movement from the Tommies, nor heard a sound."

"Good. Now get out of here and get yourself warm. You're no use as an ice pop. *Auf Wiedersehen.*"

It was the duty of a sentry to sit at the top steps of the dugout and look out from the parapet. At any sign of danger or attack, he was to alert the defenses. Franz covered himself in the blanket and adjusted his body. There was enough morning light for the spyglass to be useful. He peered out into No Man's Land. Nothing interesting, only a light dusting of snow that covered bushes and trees that had been torn to pieces by rifle bullets and shells. Some of the shell holes still had frozen corpses in them. The land was dormant, waiting to catch its breath. Just before he put the spyglass down, a large tree caught his attention.

The tree stood there solitary and ghost-like, the silent observer of a snowy field. It was an ancient tree with a thick weathered bark of pale grey. The ends of its branches moved with the whispers of the wind. Unfortunately, the tree did not escape the horrors of war; it was ravaged with scars and broken limbs. He imagined the amount of sap that dripped down the wounded bark. *What would the growth ring say if anything this year? This tree is near hell, does it realize this?*

This tree, this mighty piece of nature, had so many more years remaining to grow. The branches know only how to grow upwards towards the light of the sun. If it survives it will sprout new growth and its wounds will seal up then it will go on. Just like us when this war finally ends.

Franz covered another yawn. His eyelids grew leaden, sliding down despite every effort to keep them open. His eyes were about to close.

Franz was startled by a loud rumbling sound. He thought his heart was going to pound through his ribs. An armored vehicle climbed out of the enemy position and entered No Man's Land. This mechanical monster was a metal beast that made screeching sounds from its tracks as it jerked forward. The tank had a single turret. It reminded Franz of a picture of a charging rhino.

Franz slid down the parapet. He ran through the trench kicking anything that would make a loud noise and shouting at the top of his lungs. "Vite! Vite! Get to your positions!" The trench quickly turned into a disturbed hive, a mass of grey appeared from the dugouts and took positions. The allies began launching a constant barrage of artillery shells on the German line in an attempt to mask the attack.

Five enemy tanks spread out from the Allied lines. The lumbering vehicles moved slower than a walking man. Rifle fire opened up but would not penetrate the metal murderers. The machine gun posts opened up on the tanks. Still nothing. Allied infantry began to follow behind the cover of the tanks. As luck would have it, the allies had none. The monstrous tanks defeated themselves. Three tanks quickly stalled from mechanical issues. One was stuck in a crater unable to climb out and one was halted by a heroic soldier who was able to throw a grenade down its turret. With the tanks knocked out of battle, the advance stopped along with their supporting artillery fire; the allied infantry wisely retreated under punishing machine gunfire. They ran for their lives.

Black smoke filled the air after German artillery blew up the now useless tanks. The smell of burning petrol filled the air.

Adolf tapped Franz on the shoulder.

"Sir, no casualties or wounded from our company."

"Thank you, sergeant."

Adolf sneered. "Ach those mechanical beasts not worth a puddle of pee to the Allies if you ask me,"

Franz raised an eyebrow in thought. "If you ask me, I think we're darn lucky. But luck doesn't last forever; sooner or later it fails. They will continue to improve those mechanical contraptions till they get it right. Just a matter of time. Mark me before those metal beasts return to hurt us."

"Well, maybe you're right." Adolf tisked. "But we'll match them. I'm sure of that. With something better of our own."

"Of course we will. Then they'll match us. When does it end?"

Adolf harrumphed. "It never does. Not until we're dead on both sides."

"Isn't modern warfare fun? The natural order of war is changing forever with this new technology. Our ancestors never would have imagined those mechanical beasts. One day we may become so advanced we will kill our adversaries without even seeing them."

"Sounds like you're describing a transition from soldiering to murdering?"

Franz's voice hardened. "Maybe. Only time will tell."

Adolf kicked a small stone as he thought to change the subject. *"Huch,* you look horrible. Did Hans give you a nip of that brandy of his?"

"He did."

"Your sentry duty is over now. Get some rest, old-timer."

"Old-timer?"

"Sir, I meant to say, sir." Adolf's voice trailed off. "Sir, old-timer." Awkward silence.

Franz rolled his eyes then gave Adolf a hard slap on the shoulder. "My friend, I'd rather be an old-timer than have dirt in my mouth. When I was younger, I had a serious medical condition that meant I had to eat dirt four times a day." A short pause. "I'm lucky my older brother told me about it."

Adolf scratched his head then began to snort in laughter. His laughter flowed freely, more like a child despite his years.

Big fat snowflakes began to fall. Franz and Adolf stood up at the bottom of the trench and watched them fall. The large flakes drifted lazily from the sky. The snow began to pick up, dotting the men's clothing. As the earth began to be covered in a thick blanket of white, Franz, followed by Adolf, with the faint crunch of snow underfoot returned underground.

CHAPTER 7

SEND 'EM TO THE INFERNO

To say the cold was bitter was an understatement. It was so cold it hurt. The wind gusts stung their faces, causing them to be windburned. So cold that ice formed on the tips of their runny noses. Misery had found a good company and that good company was 1st Company under Franz's command. A motley assortment of men plucked from all walks of life. Through whatever life held before, they all shared one thing now: suffering.

Franz and his company watched the bombardment against the allied position. They watched shells rain down in a glorious show. Thunder roared as explosions erupted. Dirt, snow, and debris flew high into the air. A good hit, possibly a supply stash, a fiery yellow flame billowed out. A pillar of dark dust and fiery smoke floated above the British line. After the bombardment an eerie silence.

Whistles blew from the German line. It was their time to take the offensive to the enemy. *Here we go again*, thought Franz. *More cattle for slaughter.*

"Alright, boys, it's cold as hell out there. Let's do them a favor and send them to the inferno to warm up," Franz hollered.

The Germans sprawled out of the top of the trenches. They moved as fast as their legs would carry them. No Man's Land was quiet. The only sound was the crunching sound from their boots on the snow. A fierce crack of machine-gun fire opened up, grinding the field with bullets. All around, Franz heard men screaming and bodies falling.

"Take cover!" Franz yelled.

The Germans took what little cover they could find: craters, stumps, corpses. The Germans plodded forward at a slow advance. Like mindless zombies, they staggered forward regardless of the bullet spray.

Franz ducked down behind a blown-out tree trunk then looked around. He watched as a young baby-faced soldier took several hits and crumpled to the ground with two surrounding men next to him going down with shots to their legs. The baby-faced soldier was instantly killed; the other two moaned in agony and crawled for cover. They were pinned down. Franz paused for a moment to examine the situation. He thought to himself. *This advance is going to get us all killed. It's useless to push forward. As useless as udders on a bull. A game of chess back and forth with men as pawns.*

Franz found Hans. He grabbed him by the coat. "Sergeant, continue the advance slowly. Only a matter of time before command signals retreat. I need three men."

Hans tapped three men close by. "Go with the lieutenant."

Franz advanced towards the men that were pinned down, the three draftees close-by.

"Keep the cover fire burning for me. Shake that machine gun hive!" Using the same burned-out stump Franz used for cover previously, the three started firing at the Allied machine gun nest.

Franz crawled towards the wounded men. The three kept up a steady fire but it was not enough to halt the steady machine-gun spray. The stump was torn apart as machine-gun fire ripped into the three, rattling their bodies. Any cover fire ended with their last gurgled breath.

That machine gun nest needs to go, Franz thought. He turned from the pinned men and made his way towards the chatter of automatic weapon fire. Franz weaved across the field using holes and debris to mask his movement. The British machine gunners were firing like madmen and did not notice Franz snake toward them. Franz crawled on his hands and knees, keeping as low as possible. He slid under the barricade of barbed wire. The back of his uniform tore. He felt the wetness of blood from the cuts. He pushed on. The machine gun stopped barking as it was reloaded. Franz unclipped a grenade from his belt and threw it into the nest. He hugged the dirt.

An explosive thud. His hand screamed. A shard of flying shrapnel removed half of his index finger. The wound sent nasty jolts of pain to his brain with every millimeter of movement. He lay on his back stunned, trying to catch his breath. He thought to call out for help, but the words caught in his throat. There were others in worse shape than him and he was too close to the enemy. He could endure. He turned himself over. The bloody hand went into a patch of ice-cold snow nearby.

He rolled his eyes in pain. His mind flicked thoughts as he wrapped his hand with a field dressing he kept in his pants pocket. His dressing bled through. He reached into his pocket to pull out the dirty rag previously used for nose-blowing to stem the tide. His polished wood pipe fell out. *Why are you here with me? I ran out of tobac. Oh, what I wouldn't do to be sitting on my old chair puffing you.* He shook his head. *You don't keep it together, you're never gonna smoke that pipe again.* His thoughts drifted to memories of home. He could see images of his wife and children at play. The sound of Bach, Toccata & Fugue in D minor drifted into his mind. *da da da, da da da da dum, da da da, da da da da dum,* and for a brief moment he was at peace, but if he didn't move out quickly his peace would lead to his demise. Blood dripped from his bandaged hand making a trail of blood as he worked his way back to the German line in a crouched walk. He grew light-headed and woozy as he stumbled forward. He fainted fifty feet from the defensive wire. So close to the line he could taste it.

Retreat sounded and the Germans moved quickly back to their defensive positions. They dragged all wounded they could safely collect. Franz staggered up, spitting the dirt from his mouth and readjusting his helmet. A medic noticed the bloody makeshift wrap dripping red droplets on the white snow. Franz waved him off but the young man was persistent.

"I'm fine, get going." Franz snapped.

The medic's eyes showed that he was going to help regardless of any plea from Franz that he was fine. "Sir, I don't care about your rank. If you don't let me help you, I swear I'll knock you out and drag you back with me."

Franz nodded reluctantly.

Franz leaned on the medic. The medic grabbed Franz's good hand with his and the medic's other arm grabbed under Franz's leg. Then he hoisted Franz up over his shoulders and carried him to safety.

The bumpy journey ended at a dressing station cut deep in the ground lit with electric light. Franz waited on a wooden stool that looked like it was about to collapse under his weight. The bloody dressing was removed and the wound was exposed.

A field doctor grabbed his wounded hand with a vice grip. "Now this may sting a little. We're going to use a silver nitrate solution to cauterize your stub there."

"W-What did you say, Doc..... aah"

"There, you are as good as new. Well, missing a chunk of you."

"Thanks, Doc."

The Doc brought over a wash tray and cleaned his wound, then wrapped up his hand like a mummy. "Keep it clean. Here." He stuffed fresh bandage wrappings in Franzs' coat pocket. "In case you need another."

Hans approached. He shook his head. "How did that feel?" Before Franz could answer, Hans said, "I have the count. Including yourself, sixteen wounded and six killed in action." He cleared his throat. "Adolf didn't make it. He's a goner."

Franz sighed and shook his head. Visions of Adolf flashed through his mind. His voice croaked, "How did it happen?"

"Didn't even see it coming. Machine gun. He got hit hard. His head was almost taken clean off. Fortunately, the body did make it back. He will at least be buried like a soldier not left to decay out there." Franz trembled, visibly shaken with imagery of Adolf's death.

"Hey, you look like crap. I should let you rest."

"No time to rest. Sergeant, take a seat."

Hans removed his helmet and sat on it.

"Have the most veteran squad leader take over Adolf's platoon."

"That would be Lukas."

"The one who received his grade school teaching credentials just before he shipped off to boot camp?"

"Yes that's the one, he's up to the job I'm sure. He's young but doesn't panic under pressure, and the men like him." Han's voice turned low and grave. "Hey, let me help pen the letters to the families. We only carry so many emotional deposits in us. These are the deposits of good thoughts. I fear we will lose a little of these deposits with every letter we write to the fallen families. How many deposits do you have left?"

"I will write a letter to Adolf's family. You can help me with the rest. Hans, sorry about Adolf. I know he was a good friend of yours."

"A good friend to both of us. I'll miss his wit, I tell yah."

"It was his time. He'll be missed but we will honor him by surviving this and getting back home."

Han spoke absently, "Do you think we will make it back home?"

"We will, Hans. We will." Franz spoke with conviction but he didn't believe it. *It's a wonder any of us are still alive. If and when we return, a part of us will always be left on the battlefield.*

CHAPTER 8

GRADUATION DAY

The American army rushed to war. Despite President Woodrow Wilson's insight of the US getting dragged into the inevitable European conflict, the United States was awakening, like wind speeds building up to form a hurricane. General Pershing, who led American forces in Cuba and the Philippines and US intervention in Mexico, recently in 1916, would command the US forces. The storm of American resolve would be challenged to build a million-man army. Within 6 months, hundreds of construction projects needed to be built, including sewage, hospitals, railroad spurs, and military posts, and everything needed to operate smoothly. Equipment for the soldiers was another bottleneck. Waves of men were forced to drill with wooden rifles and had little actual target practice because of ammunition shortages. The Americans were desperately unprepared but through sheer will the brave but half-trained amateurs would take on the fight, ready or not.

Myles was sent to boot camp at Fort Devens, Massachusetts. Finished in October 1817, it was named after a Union Civil War Major General, Charles Devens. The Fort's location was valuable due to its connection to the rail network in New England. The Fort was a virtual boomtown that grew overnight and it could barely contain the activity present. It was the task of the Fort command to take the raggle-taggle young men that came in and spit them out as a cohesive unit. They succeeded. Every man was trained to obey orders, even the most inconceivable command. They held a little less humanity now, replaced by cold instruments of war. Everyone at the top command knew the recruiters may never return and that they could end up shattered and drunk old men, but they needed obedient soldiers to enter the hellfire of war they were being sent to.

Myles's mind and physique went through a significant change since joining the army. When he first arrived, his workouts would have left his arms empty and a rising feeling of nausea in his stomach. After weeks spent in arduous exercises, he was now a pillar of health. Evidence of his physical accomplishment was in his weight. With plenty of food and exercise, he packed on ten pounds of solid muscle. His mind was shaped to the discipline of daily military life. It took no will to get up at 5:30 in the morning to run three miles before the day started. Mind and body were crafted into a military machine. A machine built for one purpose, to bleed for his country.

"Get down and give me twenty-five," snapped the Drill Sergeant Campbell, a heavyset man in his early late forties with touches of grey in his hair. He looked like he ate nuts and bolts for breakfast. Myles sank to his knees then stretched out in a pushup position. He pumped out his pushups with ease.

"Don't yah think because graduation's tomorrow I'll ease up on you?" A glint of devilry in Campbell's eyes. "Now give me 50 sit-ups!"

Myles completed the sit-ups. *I wonder if Sarg has ever done any in his life?* Myles barely broke a sweat.

Sergeant Cambell noticed as well. "Now give me some squats, twenty-five". Myles groaned.

After the squats, Myles stood up, beaming with confident eyes.

"So you think you can slack off? Not on my watch. Wash this floor again and if it doesn't shine like the top of the Woolworth building you'll be lapping the barracks till you drop."

"Yes, Drill Sergeant," hollered Myles. Myles ran off to fetch a mop and bucket. Sergeant Cambell cracked a smile at Myles' back.

Graduation day was held on a beautiful sunny day. Myles stood with a large mass of soldiers in front of a wooden podium to hear long and boring speeches from the fort's commanders.

Sweat rolled down the back of his neck and back. He was dressed in his woolen, issued uniform, uncomfortable at best in the warm sun. Although wool does a great job absorbing perspiration, it feels as heavy as carrying lead bricks around with you in the heat of the sun. The physical torture would be over when the fort commander finished the ceremony with a speech of his own. Myles gazed over the crowd looking for his family and Kathy. He spotted them. His parents, Lilly, and Kathy were sitting next to each other dressed in their Sunday best. Kathy sat next to his mother wearing a dress he had never seen her wear before, made of green corduroy with large collars that framed her shoulders. A shiver ran down his back as his thoughts drifted to embracing her. *When is this torture going to end? I'm ready for combat but this is too much. I'm surprised only one has passed out in formation. Don't lock your legs or you'll join 'em.*

The fort commander, Major General Harry F. Hodges, approached the podium.

"Welcome, men, to the 76th U.S. Infantry Division. General Pershing wanted health and physical strength, endurance, smartness, and active precision above all else and I believe we have delivered this to him. You men are proficient in the bayonet and able to hit a target up to 600 yards away. The Huns will flee if they know what's good for them. You follow in a tradition of the American army that is handed down from the days of Valley Forge under Baron Von Steuben. In those early days citizen soldiers trained to fight for the cause of liberty and freedom. Now men are needed once again to take up that fight. Evil is trying to plant itself and destroy democracy. I am proud of you men and the sacrifice you are willing to make. Know that we will gain inevitable triumph for your efforts—so help us, God. Commanders bring your men to attention." A shout of "battalion," followed by "company," followed by "platoon," rang out. Hodges saluted the men. "Dismissed!"

Myles's heart palpated jubilation as the crowd erupted in applause. He followed the wave of soldiers to the stands.

Mary gave him a warm hug and a fat kiss on his forehead. "I'm proud of you, son. You left us my little boy now you're a man."

Lilly gave him a poke to his chest and smiled. "Jeez, you packed on some weight. What have they been feeding you?"

"Mostly milk and cookies," Myles said in a serious voice.

"Very funny!"

Frank squeezed Myles's hand in a hearty handshake. "Not so long ago you were playing baseball. You've grown up. Your bat has been switched for a rifle. But know this, you can grow up all you want but you'll always be my kid and you will never beat me at chess."

"Maybe I'll find a way to practice while I'm away. Meet a chess champion to show me some moves, then come back and wallop yah."

Frank harrumphed. "Keep dreaming."

Mary motioned to Kathy. "Now you guys don't take all day. It's a long way back and you never know if the T will have trouble. I'm amazed we only had to stop twice on the way up."

The family troop walked away, leaving Kathy beside Myles.

Kathy held Myles's hand. "My parents wanted to congratulate you and my sisters, especially Martha." Martha was a nine-year-old that held a great fondness for Myles. It could be called a crush. Kathy tousled Myles's dark brown hair that had been cut short. "You sure look handsome in uniform," she smiled. "A fine-looking doughboy," she teased.

"I thought I looked great in anything," Myles joked. "Not everyone can look as good as you in whatever they wear."

Kathy blushed. "Before I forget. I gotcha something." She handed him a photo of herself. She ran her hand over his back as he looked at it. He turned over the photo to find a handwritten note on the back. **"Come back safe to me."**

Myles looked deep into Kathy's eyes. Her eyes and face showed what her voice hid. Eyes a deep pool hiding an ocean of endless emotion. The fear is evident by the crease of her brow and the curve of her lips. Myles moved his head close to Kathy. His lips brushed her ear as he spoke. "Kathy" he choked. "You know I'm coming back." They embraced.

She let her body sag and her muscles became loose. As he cradled her she felt her worries lose their sting. He leaned in for a kiss. She pulled back.

"You know, Myles?"

He cleared his throat. "Yes?"

"You better not mess with those French girls over there. They say French is the language of love. You best not be given any."

Myles laughed out loud. "Doesn't matter what language they speak, they'll have nothing on you. Besides, my heart is spoken for."

She kissed him on the lips.

"Kathy, I promise to write to you as often as possible."

"I promise to write to you all the time. My heart will grow fonder waiting for you. I know you didn't want to give me a ring before you left, but I'm waiting for one when you return."

"Kathy, you know—Hey."

Lilly tugged Myles's hand. "Come on, guys. Ma and Dad are gonna take us all out for ice cream before we leave. No more smacking lips, ya hear me?"

"Ok, Lilly. We're done."

Kathy winked. "Well…" She gave Myles a final kiss on the lips. "Now we're ready."

"We all scream, we all scream for ice cream," cried Lilly.

Ice cream and sunshine are not always the greatest combination. But even melted, the treat that was once reserved only for royalty, is delicious. It has one of the highest likability ratings out of any food. Who do you know that doesn't enjoy ice cream? Sweet ice cream and Kathy's kiss would be Myles's final memory before he departed to war. He savored them both.

CHAPTER 9

DOUGHBOYS SET SAIL

Americans, nicknamed "doughboys," were arriving in Europe in great numbers. The term Doughboy was first used during the American Civil War when Cavalrymen used the term to make fun of foot soldiers. They teased that the brass buttons on infantry uniforms looked like dough cakes or flour dumplings, or the term may have originated because of the flour or pipeclay which the soldiers used to brighten the whites on their uniforms. However they received their name, the doughboys were indeed a lifeline given to the Allies that were limping along. The first waves of American soldiers landed in the spring of 1918. They were late to the fight but not too late to make a difference.

The Allies were close to losing the war with Germany. Already, France had lost 3 million men and Britain 2 million. The French Army was in open rebellion with half of its fighting force refusing to attack the Germans. The British prime minister Lloyd George feared a social revolution in his country if casualties continued to mount. At the end of 1917, a total of 800,000 British were lost, the nadir being an epic failure during a 3-month assault of the muddy heights of Passchendaele where 300,000 fell to gain a pathetic two miles of ground. The German Empire on the other hand was getting stronger. After success in Russia and Italy, they were deploying 100 fresh divisions and would outnumber the allies on the western front by over a million.

It was now August 1918, and a continuous wave of American transports was arriving in Europe. Every ship that could be serviced was fitted for carrying troops. Myles was on a convoy sent from New York traveling to Port of Brest, France. With the threat of German submarines, the transport and supply convoy was escorted by the cruiser USS Seattle, destroyers USS Roe, Terry, Wilkes, and the converted as well as armed yacht Corsair. The convoy zigzagged across the water, trying not to make target practice for German submarines. It was no pleasure cruise for the passengers. The full duration of the trip, nearly two weeks, passengers came up on deck only once or twice a day, usually for brief exercise, lifeboat drill, or to hurl over the sides.

Dark grey clouds covered the sky blocking out most of the sun. The USS Tenadores bobbed up and down in the rough ocean. The strong smell of brine lingered in the strong breeze. Myles gripped the railing of the steamship so tightly that tendons stood out on the backside of his fist. The pitching and rolling of the ship gave nausea that bubbled in his gut, turning his stomach sour. His face went deathly pale. Over the railing of the steamer went whatever contents were in his stomach. He wretched over and over again. Emptying his stomach was supposed to make him feel better. It did not. He sweated profusely and felt weak as a newborn lamb. He spewed over the side again.

"You gonna be alright there?" Sergeant Perkins asked, the concern clear in her voice. "Never seen someone turn as white as you did. Kinda looked like a corpse."

"Thanks," muttered Myles.

Sergeant Lance Perkins was Myle's platoon sergeant. Lance was one of the few with military experience before the war. He was a former member of the Massachusetts National Guard who, like many, answered the call to service. Despite his age (Lance was only 28), he had a grey streak running down his short hair. His love of food gave him a robust frame. His eyes were as dark as coal. He was a favorite of the men because of his carefree attitude and tongue. He would not constrain his tongue even for officers. If he had, he would likely be a higher rank than he was. Lance simply did not care.

"I think my stomach may have followed the food over the side, sarge," Myles moaned.

"Well, it's owned by the Army. Now better get it back or they'll court-martial you for losing it." Lance laughed at his own joke. "Ship should be arriving at port soon. All in one piece. So far those demon subs didn't get us. Make sure you add prayers of thanks for that."

"You bet, sarge," Myles said, glad to change the subject. "There's a lot of prayers going out on either side. Both sides read the same Bible and pray to the same God. Both request his divine providence. How do you think he chooses who to answer?"

"Who do you think I am? A priest. I can't tell you. I do like to think there is a reason for all the crap going on over there. We're all on our way to this crap. But crap or not, I can't wait to see France."

"Well, I'd like to see any place with dried land. Myles yawned. "I can't recall when I last had a good night's sleep."

Lance smiled. "I hear the food is great. Home of warm bread and cheese. The home of letting them eat cake."

Myles's stomach dry heaved.

"Oh sorry, talk of food later," Lance said crisply.

"Gentlemen, enjoying the view?" A ship's officer in a new blue service coat with a stiff turndown collar and a black tie approached.

"Sir," Lance and Myles spoke at the same time.

"At ease. Commander James B. Gilmer at your service. I see your friend doesn't have his sea legs yet. Many of you land lovers never venture to the sea. You don't know what you're missing." Commander

Gilmer motioned to Myles with a grin. "You look as white as a ghost. Take heart, we will be landing soon."

"Soon won't be quick enough," mumbled Myles.

"What do you think of this ship?" James did not wait for a reply. "Ah, ain't she a beauty, built-in 1913 in Belfast to service a fruit company. You would never imagine it would be taken over by the US navy and hurriedly fitted. She's a good girl although she gets moody on the water sometimes. Be glad she's heavy, now she doesn't bob as much."

"Oh I just love this ship, I just can't wait to get off her. That's all," Myles spoke with a hint of sarcasm.

"If you would oblige me, let me share a valuable tip. Look toward the horizon. It will help. Here, this will help also." Gilmer pulled from his pocket a white, wrapped paper. He unfolded it and displayed a couple of red and white swirled candies. "Here, take one."

Myles picked one and put it into his mouth. A cool peppermint sensation tickled his throat. After a few seconds, he crunched the peppermint then swallowed it.

"Thank you. It does seem to help some."

"You're welcome." Gilmore touched the brim of his hat. "Good day, gentlemen; if you travel again, be sure to stay with us."

"Well, it's been a pleasure, but I do hope not to be on a ship for a while."

"On the contrary, let's hope it's not that long. A lot of nasty business over in France. When it's over, you may embrace any ship regardless of erratic motion if it means you have a ticket home. Stay safe."

Myles watched Gilmore depart. He thought out loud, "I wonder if he speaks the truth?"

"Wonder why he didn't offer me any fancy peppermints, then again I haven't had my face over the railing," Lance teased. "Hey, I'm going to grab some chow. I don't think you'll be interested. Why don't you go below and rest a bit."

Myles made his way to the cramped, warm, and damp billeted area on the ship's lower deck. The men were packed in like sardines. The foul smell of unchecked body odor permeated the air. The men hadn't showered since they left New York. He squeezed through the swarm of men to his hammock. The noise level was deafening with all talking at once. *How am I going to rest with all this racket and get my mind off this infernal boat motion? Maybe a visit with Betsy.*

He fetched his rifle he nicknamed Betsy then he sat back down on his hammock. He pulled out a dirty rag and a tiny bottle of oil from his cloth bandolier that was stuffed next to several empty magazines. Betsy was wiped off then caressed with a thin coating of oil. The oil would help protect his newly issued Springfield rifle model 1903 that had never been shot, from the elements. Up until now, it had been mostly dust. He looked forward to breaking in the weapon in France where they were promised plenty of ammunition.

The whistle sounded for the evening meal and the surrounding hammocks became quieter. Myles opened a flap of his olive drab canvas rucksack. Inside the stuffed flap were bread rations, a baking tin, a condiment can, and his Bible. He pulled out his Bible then sat cross-legged on his hammock. He lifted up the thread marking where he left off his last page, in the chapter of John. The pocket Bible was a gift from his mother before he left. He promised her that he would continue to read the Word daily. He kept his word at Bootcamp and onboard the ship although it was difficult to read with the lighting and the noise. He read.

Myles finished reading after the passage from John 13:34: *"A new command I give you: Love one another. As I have loved you, so you must love one another."* He pondered the meaning. His thoughts brought him to remember when Jesus was asked directly what are the most important commandments to follow? *Jesus answered, 'First Love God with all your might then love your neighbor.' Love your neighbor? Does this apply to war? Surely not. The Germans are the devil on earth, evil incarnate. They deserve what is coming. It isn't murdering. It's not sinful to kill in war if the war is just.* He tucked the Bible back in his rucksack. *On the very day of his arrest, Jesus said to his disciples. 'If you don't have a sword, sell your cloak and buy one.' He knows we need to defend ourselves from evil aggressors.*

Myles turned on his back then sprawled out on his hammock. He pulled out a collection of 7 small photos from his breast pocket. One of his Mom and Dad, one of his Grandfather, two of his beloved Shilo, his Staffordshire terrier mix, two of his kid sister Lilly, and the picture Kathy gave him. He flipped through the photos, stopping at Kathy's. A brief smile stretched across his face. He loved her. He was determined to propose when he returned after the war. He was not a fool. He understood an enemy of love was distance. *I hope it's true that absence makes the heart grow stronger. I hope my grandfather is right.* He placed the photos back.

Myles had to take everything out from a different flap of his rucksack. This one was stuffed with a towel, shaving kit, soap dish, foot powder, and extra socks to locate his folded letters sent from home. For a brief period, he could escape home with the words on a page.

Across the sleeping quarters, a soldier pulled out a harmonica and started to play. The sound the music produced was comforting. Myles followed the melody as the player blew into the harmonica. He lost himself in the melody with its subdued intensity. No longer fixed on a page, his mind relaxed. Under the swaying of the boat and the melody of a harmonica, Myles nodded off.

Myles dreamed. He stood alone at his favorite beach spot in Narragansett, Rhode Island. The air of the briny ocean water filled his nose. Sounds of gulls laughing on shore tickled his ear. He was shirtless and dressed in shorts. His bare toes sunk into the grainy sand. He watched the breaking waves crash along the shore rocks.

His attention turned to a magnificent sailboat gliding through the water. It blinked out and in its place, a German U-boat appeared. A giant imperial flag waved in the breeze near the periscope. This white flag depicted a single-headed black eagle against a circle surrounded by a large black cross. The left corner of the flag depicted a black cross over black, white, and red horizontal stripes. Three sailors were loading a shell for the deck gun. His limbs froze. He scanned the water for the target. Nothing. He looked along the shoreline.

A young family was enjoying themselves upon primrose sand. A young boy and a girl were building castles in the sand. The mother and father were laying backside on a large blanket enjoying the sun's rays oblivious to the danger.

Myles ran towards them. "Germans! Get out! Run!" He expected them to scramble and run for it but the family ignored his cries for help. As he got closer he noticed the father's face was a perfect reflection of himself. The mother's face was an image of Kathy. He paused in shock. The cannon fired.

Myles woke. The harmonica had stopped playing and it was pitch dark. He caught the distinct scent of a match struck and the orange glow of a lit cigarette along with an acrid stench. A few hammocks over Lance inhaled.

Myles kept his voice low. "Hey, Lance?"

"Hey, kid, how's your stomach? You've got those sea legs yet?" Lance slid off his hammock and stood before Myles. He sucked in a long drag from his cigarette and blew a cloud of smoke toward the ceiling. "You looked like a sleeping beauty. I was not so lucky to sleep, I miss my nice soft bed and I can't get that dang harmonica racket out of my head either."

Myles smirked. "I kinda liked the music. My stomach is fine, but let's face it, I may never get my sea legs."

"You would make a poor sailor, there's no doubt about that in my book."

Myles yawned and stretched his arms up. "Darn hammock. I bet a bed of nails is probably more comfortable. Don't worry, I would never dream of being a sailor. I'm curious, what did you do for work before joining up?"

"I fiddled with cows," Lance chuckled. "A peaceful life I reckon, a lot of hard work for little money. Up every morning at the crack of dawn. Never a day off. I have a family to support, a wife, and four children. All boys. My oldest son is named Robert. He's twelve and he's a great help. The man of the house while I'm away. My wife is going to need every ounce of help running our farm while I'm gone. Sometimes I feel like I'm on vacation here. I get to sleep in on occasion. Have three square meals a day. Hey, why do you ask? You don't want to be a farmer, do you?"

"Just curious, that's all. Not sure what I want to do, sailoring is definitely out of the running. I can't see myself sitting with a piece of straw between my teeth milking a cow either. But both are more exciting than what awaits me. I'll probably be stuck bored out of my mind working at a mill. My options are limited when we get back to the states, but I definitely want to consider."

"When we get back. Hmm. Are you ready for the western front, Myles? I never fought. I was too young for the Spanish-American war but I heard the stories. We kicked butt for the United States and all, yet it wasn't all fun and games for the guys that came back. Soldering ain't bad. Well, it can suck being outside and dealing with the weather. If it ain't raining we ain't training, but it's taking another man's life that's hard and living with it. I have a few friends who are vets. They told me initially you may feel exhilarated with a kill and think little of it, but later, after the bullets stop flying, emotions may creep up on you. Whatever sins we commit they're gonna give us scars. Scars that cut deep."

"You're getting kind of deep there."

"So I am. Must be moody. Thinking of subs firing on us. Don't want to end up at the bottom of the ocean. Whatever happens, when we arrive it's shite we have no control over. After it's over, whatever you choose for work, pick something that makes you happy. If you ever want to diddle with cows, let me know." Lance extinguished the nearly finished cigarette on a metal pipe of the ship. "Now get yourself some rest, Myles, I have a feeling we're gonna need all we can get."

"Sure thing".

Metal moaned in a long exasperated breath. The floor listed sharply. Lance grabbed a nearby metal pol. He hung tightly in a death grip. An alarm bell rang. Men lurched awake in a panic to stagger out of their hammocks. His face grew pale. He imagined inhaling briny water into the abyss. Lance's fear of a sub attack had been realized. People have an odd way of thinking of death. It's usually ugly, but the fear of drowning can rattle the deepest anxieties.

Duty snapped Lance out of his temporary trance. He yelled, "Asses up. We've been hit. Get on deck! Move now, if you stay here you'll wake up with clouds surrounding you and heavenly music."

Not looking back, Lance headed to the stairs.

Myles slid from his hammock and followed Lance. The ship's crew and passengers stirred into motion like a hornet's nest stuck with a knife.

The door to the deck was open revealing the early morning light. After the last step taking Lance on deck, he slipped. Losing his balance, he fell hitting the deck hard, face first. He raised his head. His mouth was covered in blood and a front tooth was missing. Myles moved Lance from blocking the escaping passengers.

Lance moved to a sitting position then looked at the blood on his hands. "Shoot," he gurgled in pain.

"Medic!" Cried Myles.

Captain Gilmore approached and took a knee. "Are you men alright?"

"Sergeant Perkins slipped and whacked his face. He plum lost a tooth."

"Anything to the face always looks worse than it is. Here." He handed them a clean white handkerchief from his coat pocket. Lance held it to his mouth. The cloth quickly soaked in red. "You can keep it. No need to panic. We are lucky. The torpedo hit the port side of the ship. Bastards destroyed the propulsion unit. Granted we are sitting ducks but we are not going to sink. No water was taken." He pointed to Myles. "Get him to sickbay. Go!"

A quick trip to sickbay and Lance found his mouth full of gauze and misery.

"Hey, you look good, Sarge. It's an improvement."

Lance looked at Myles with dagger eyes. "What do you mean? I'm missing a friggin' tooth."

"It gives you character."

"Yeah, it says I'm an idiot."

Returning to the billet area they found the crew packing for the transfer to the armored cruiser USS Tennessee. Tennessee was available from its return trip from Europe. It pulled alongside the crippled Tenadores and began an evacuation of the nonessential ship's crew and passengers. The passengers were forced to sleep in the billeting area onboard, but at least they did not sleep with the fishes.

Soon the USS Tennessee would be arriving in France. Myles would see if his daydreams of combat and heroics would manifest to reality. Myles also understood war was no picnic, but the young man was naive to what truly awaited him. His Grandfather carried the scars of war without ever fighting. Scars that carried the sorrow of war, a three-letter word that can reap destruction on us all. This great war would be a battle of Goliath against Goliath, and both sides had all the toys. It was no old-fashioned battle with courageous young men lining up to fire on their enemies. It was a modern war with machine guns and accurate artillery. The carnage that awaited could cut deep scars.

CHAPTER 10

CHALLENGE OF THE TOMMIES

The grey clouds moved off and the sun came out to shine above USS Tennessee. Out of its large smokestacks, puffs of grey smoke drifted lazily, dissipating into the still summer air. The sea was perfectly calm as the brine parted from the ship's bow sending white foam cascading to the side. Sea birds soared across the sky with their silhouettes dark against the bright sky. In what felt like an eternity to the passengers a long whistle blew, signaling land ahead.

The crowded ship was a swarm of activity. Soldiers packed up their few personal items and military gear then stood on deck watching the shore approach. The click of their shoes could be heard as they shuffled on deck. They wore the newly issued Russel-marching shoes, sometimes referred to as little tanks because of the attached iron plates at the heels.

The cruiser docked at the Port of Brest. A large crowd of civilians gathered to welcome the doughboys. It was a carnival-like atmosphere as the troops departed the ship. The French people were delirious with joy; they saw hope that the war would end quickly with the Americans there. The crowd near the docks sang joyful songs to the arriving soldiers in broken English.

The arriving American force did not linger; they joined the established American Expeditionary Force, still in the process of setting up communication and supply networks at training camps miles in the rear. Also in the rear, charitable organizations including the American Red Cross, the Knights of Columbus, the YMCA, and other organizations were set up to provide little comforts that would make life on the front more tolerable.

Experienced French and English instructors taught them how to survive in trench warfare at the camps. Full demonstration platoons with combat veterans were also available. Soon the American troops would visit quiet sectors in the front lines to become familiar with conditions there, then temporarily each American unit would be attached to a corresponding French unit. The Americans had yet to see combat; nonetheless, they were excited to begin. There was a general opinion among the American army to get the war over with.

Someone said to an instructor, "Let's get on with it, there's nothing more you can teach us, so far from the action where there's something doing. We don't want to stay forever, where are the goddamn Germans?"

"Just over there!" the instructor replied. "You'll know where they are soon enough when they start throwing shells about! Don't be so cocksure about your souvenirs until the fight is over."

In a small clearing just outside training camp, named twenty-two, near a dirt road under the shade of chestnut and oak trees, Myles's platoon rested after chow provided by a French mess. They had indulged in corn beef the French called bully beef, root vegetables, and biscuits. To their amazement, they were given sweet desserts and wine with their meal. Most of the time doughboys lived on canned meat, hard bread, and instant coffee or the newly developed Emergency Ration, either a cake of powdered wheat and meat or a chocolate one. This meal was an unexpected feast. Under the shade of trees, the men relaxed. Muscles that had been toiling hard were now asked to vegetate.

A cloud of dust came down the road as a long column of British soldiers began to march by. A British division was rotating out of the trenches to recharge. The slang for the British soldiers was 'Tommies' after a fictitious private Tommy Atkins in a popular 1892 song. A few Americans began to stagger up to watch the British column pass. A few verbal teases passed back and forth. The teases led to a shouting match of insults.

One particular British officer, a thin as a rail captain with a mole on his chin, scoffed at the Americans and arrogantly retorted, "The mickey isn't yet out of their boasting, they only got to arrive and knock Jerry out. They'll realize that even their tin helmets won't stop bullets! These yanks aren't so smart. Such par's. They fought the Revolutionary War over taxes now their bloody well taxed to hell."

Myles listened to the arrogant officer and could not resist the banter. "I thought we fought the war over getting rid of the yoke of the monarchy. It looks like you blokes continue to suffer from that bondage. Your monarchy's like a sickness that ain't going away."

"Blimey, didn't you Americans fight a great war over bondage? We needed no civil war to end slavery. We do what's right. Well, monarchy or not we stick together. You're all pogey-bait."

Myles snickered. "Like you stuck together at Yorktown and 1812?"

An American infantry column moving in the opposite direction of the British Captain stopped to see what the fuss was about. Myles and the British officer were surrounded by a sea of onlookers.

The British captain licked his lips before speaking. "So you think you're better than us. How about you challenge his majesty's men? Perhaps a game of football or as you Americans call it, soccer. The losing team will sing the other country's national anthem. I'd love nothing better than to hear you Americans sing God save the King."

Myles rolled his eyes, "Oh, and we'd love to hear you say the land of the free and home of the brave. We'll take that challenge!" The surrounding American soldiers echoed "Hoorah" along with other shouts of agreement.

The Captain waited for the noise to quiet then grunted back. "Alright, Yanks, Let's battle."

The American and British infantry mobilized quickly. A nearby field was hastily prepared for the game. It would be half the size of a regulation field. Wooden stakes were stuck in the ground to simulate goal posts. They dragged a pickaxe across the field to make the borders of the boundaries, then the teams were picked. The ball, a bunch of rags (an extra shirt tied with some twine), was made for the match. Those with at least some experience were chosen. Rank did not matter. The British had a major on their team and the Americans a lieutenant colonel. A robust Myles was picked to play, the scrawny Captain was not chosen. Time was a luxury; they did not have to play the game. The team that scored the first five goals would be declared the winner. A large mass of soldiers surrounded the field to cheer on the game. The voices of the crowd were blaring.

The game started. It appeared the field held hidden patches of mud. Members on both teams slipped as they jogged onto the field. The ball was tossed in the middle of the field and it was kicked back and forth at first. It was like watching an elementary school game. Complete disorder prevailed. The Tommies scored the first goal then quickly scored a second. It was clear they had more players that understood the game and they worked together to try and take a quick victory.

Myles trapped the ball with his foot, then took off dribbling the ball past two defenders. He kicked the ball straight and true, resulting in a score. The American spectators erupted in celebration. Running back to take a defensive position, he slid on the ground kicking up mud and dirt. He stood up then combed his fingers through his hair, brushing out the muck as the American crowd continued their hoots and hollers. The British took advantage during the excessive celebration and scored quickly. They led 3-1.

While the ball was retrieved by the American goalie, an American major on the team raised his arms and motioned for his teammates to huddle. His face gave him a stern appearance along with his long-boned face, tapering to a pointed chin. He pointed at Myles. Cleared his throat. "New strategy, get the ball to this one. He's the only one that seems to have a clue. Has anyone played this game on a team other than the play yard? Three men raised their hands. "Congrats! You will block for him. Everyone else, you need to kick the ball to them. I ain't going to be stuck singing 'God save the King.'" He motioned to Myles. "Now go with the blockers. Go!"

The Doughboy goalie overthrew the ball, which resulted in giving it back to the Tommies. Myles, with the blockers nearby, waited for the ball to arrive. It wasn't looking well for his team. They struggled to get the ball to him. The Tommies scored again. One more game point and the game was over. Myles looked exasperated while sweating. The sweat rolled down, cleaning lines on his dirty face. *Dang, It's over. There's no way my team is gonna get the ball to us. We're gonna be stuck singing their anthem.*

The ball soared through the air like a popup baseball. Myles ran to the ball as it bounced towards him. The defenders circled around him. He dribbled towards the goal stakes. The goalie gave him an icy stare and sneered. Myles kicked. The ball flew just over the head of the goalie. A score. The crowd cheered.

The Tommies fought hard to score again. Luck turned against them when the ball flew back towards Myles. It was a race to the ball. Myles won the race one step ahead. He gave the ball a light kick towards the goal. The Tommie chasing the ball stopped then fell hard in the dirt. Another Tommie quickly approached, getting past the doughboy defenders. *I won't dribble,* Myles thought. *He's on me like flies on a pig roast, but I bet I can outrun them. The Tommies have been in the trenches too long.* He gave the ball a soft kick. Myles was correct in his thought, just barely, he caught up to the ball with the Tommie a step behind him, then he walloped the ball. The goalie dove and missed. *Score!*

The next point scored was not done by the doughboys, but the doughboys received the point. The Tommies goaltender tried to hurl the ball out into the field but slipped and managed to knock the ball back to score one for the doughboys.

The doughboys huddled together. The major pointed at Myles again. "By the way, what's your name, son?

"It's Myles, sir."

"It's tied now. You may be our hero if you can manage one more. Myles, as my grandmother used to say, they're watching you like a hawk. Let's use that. This time head to the center of the field. We'll get you the ball. Just as you get the ball, make it look like you're going to kick it hard then instead pass the ball to one of your blockers. Let them have a go at a goal. The Tommies won't see it coming. Move out!"

A Tommie stayed glued to Myles like a mother goose watching her gosling. Myles thought quickly and said, "Look over there. I can't believe my eyes, General Pershing, to see us!"

The defender took the bait. "Where? I don't see him."

Myles sprinted to the middle of the field. The defender was way behind when he figured out the deception. Myles trapped the ball. The defenders all bolted towards him. He reared back, about to kick the ball hard straight and true. He gave it a light tap and passed the ball to one of his blockers. The blocker took off with it and kicked with a large hanging curve. It bounced off the goalie's foot, sending it through the goalposts.

Victory! The American crowd erupted and charged the field hollering and screaming and shouting, "Hoorah! Hoorah!"

The British captain that started all the fun approached Myles shaking his head in disbelief. "Captain Montgomery at your service. My friends call me Monty. You yanks beat us square." He held out his hand. Myles shook it. "Not the craziest match we ever played. We went against the Hun in what some call a Christmas Eve miracle in 1914." He furrowed his brow in thought. "The rounds stopped and the lines crossed. The orders to stop fighting did not come from superiors but the common soldiers' hearts. We laughed, joked, swapped rations. I'd trade our blood sausages any day for good German sausage. A makeshift ball appeared from somewhere, I don't know where, but I'm sure it came from their side. We made up some goals and kicked the ball around. Command was angry about the unofficial truce but we don't know of any punishments handed out. Too many to convict I think, and if word got back home about it. . . ." He harrumphed. "You fellows are good. You beat some experienced players. Jack and Oliver over there." He motioned to him. "Played in a club before the war. They're a bit rusty I guess. You Americans were lucky." He smirked. "Luck or not. If you Americans can kick the Hun like that, we're all coming home soon."

Myles feigned a frown. "Home soon? I hope it's not too early. I'm looking forward to fighting them."

"Looking forward? Anyone who craves war ought to be locked up. Just remember. Be a hero on the soccer field not on the battlefield. No one remembers you when you're under the ground. Do your job, but remember your second mission is to make it home to your family. Don't cross a minefield when you can go around it."

Myles rubbed his hand across his face. "You're right. Just want to do my duty. That's all."

"If you're in uniform, you will." Monty cast his eyes to the game field. "You're lucky I didn't play. I was hit by a sniper in the First Battle of Ypres. A nasty injury. They thought I wouldn't make it. Would you believe they even prepared a grave for me?"

Awkward silence. Myles broke it.

"Next time we play I expect you to be in the game."

"That's a promise. Thinking of promises, I believe we owe you something?"

The defeated British players stood in a row attempting the American national anthem. Hardly any knew the lyrics. Even if they had, the song is challenging at best. Ironically, the tune to the lyrics of "The Star-Spangled Banner" was stolen from an English drinking song called "To Anacreon in Heaven." It was a sight to see. The memory would stay for those that witnessed it forever. When the attempted American anthem was concluded, the British marched off in a cloud of dust trying to sing Yankee Doodle.

CHAPTER 11

GOD MUST LOVE IDIOTS

It is said that war is hell. This is the truth of it, an endless series of torments that never end. When battle listlessness set in, Franz worked to redirect his frame of mind. His men counted on his head to remain sharp and centered. Besides images of his loved ones, he redirected his brain with one of the few positive stories of the war that he personally witnessed five months into the war. No matter what dark mood clouded his head the thoughts of that day would always light his heart and bring if not a smile at least a crack of one.

It was December 24, 1914, after several weeks of mild yet soaking weather. A hard frost appeared, creating a dusting of white as if a thin layer of powdered sugar decorated the Western Front. The spirits in the trenches were high. On both sides, men thought the war would be over soon and they would soon be home with their families. The common soldiers in Franz's division had illuminated their trenches as the evening set. They sang and made merry. They also could hear the enemy across the battle lines had done so as well. If they listened closely, they could hear "The First Noel" from the British positions.

On Christmas day Franz, a sergeant at this time, was ordered to lead a reconnaissance patrol to inspect the enemy defenses. The commanders assumed as long as the patrol did not get too close, because of the holiday, no shots would be fired. What they spied out that day was a Scottish guard, a private Morker, in No Man's Land. A pencil-thin youth with a face burned red by the cold wind. His eyes radiated a warmth that can not be described properly. He approached the patrol with his hands up. He spoke in perfect German. "Don't shoot! We caught your Fritz's music last night. We could hear the piping of piccolos to 'Silent Night.' Seeing that maybe you're feeling the spirit of brotherly love and goodwill towards men, we would like to parley."

"We?" Franz said as he lowered his rifle.

"The enemy," Morker winked. "I am their spokesman. Not the entire army my friends, but at least the poor blokes directly across from you."

"Parley. Hmm. What did you have in mind?"

"Well, first we'd like to swap some rations. We're sick of the crap we've been eating. You must feel the same. But something new will surely titillate our taste buds, and secure a cease-fire for at least the remainder of the day. Let's have no rifles today. Let's go out with slices of bread and butter instead."

Franz thought and as he did a large cloud momentarily passed over the sun, temporarily dimming it. He looked up at the cloud. It was a brilliantly white, puffy cloud with smokey edges. He followed the patterns, convincing himself the cloud looked like folded hands in prayer. *Is my mind playing tricks on me? A sign? Perhaps sent from an angel above or am I just seeing what I want to see?*

Franz directed his attention to Morker. "That can be arranged. If you don't fire on us we won't fire on you. We will spread the word throughout our division." Franz winced. "I hope I don't get shot or hung for this."

"You have a deal." Morker shook Franz's hand. "Do you gentlemen have anything to trade on you now? What would you give for my mum's shortbread?" Morker pulled out a blue-colored tin box. "Well, whatcha got men?"

"I have a bottle of whiskey," a voice cried out.

"I have a few cigars," said another.

"Sold to the man with the whiskey!"

The exchange was made.

Franz and the patrol quickly spread the word of the truce. It spread like wildfire through a dry forest. Later the British and Germans in that particular combat sector crossed the lines and word of the truce continued to spread. Across the entire western front, a widespread unofficial ceasefire began. Men fraternized, exchanged food and souvenirs, there were prisoner swaps, even joint burial ceremonies. The most memorable images were from football matches, referred to as soccer in the states. Command from both sides considered this all improper and the following year it was prohibited. What happened that Christmas day may never occur again in man's history, but for the soldiers that participated in that Christmas miracle, it would forever live in their memories as an example that men can find peace and goodwill towards one another even in times of war.

Top commanders gave a blind eye, thinking the men were foolish. They couldn't punish stupidity. But were the common soldiers on both sides really being so foolish? Franz often wondered: *After a thunderclap like that beautiful display of brotherly love, how did we go back so quickly to killing one another? Oh, how God must consider us idiots. We're like sheep always losing sight of the shepherd.*

The memory of that Christmas was fading. The fighting was overly bitter now, it was difficult on both sides to look at their enemies the same way that they did that Christmas day so long ago. They were enemies, that was true, but they were brothers that understood the hell of war.

CHAPTER 12

FURRY FRIEND

The light from the sun shone brightly over a few puffy white clouds brushed on a nearly cloudless blue sky. Winter was over and now the blessings of warm weather reigned. Regardless of the weather being cold or hot, the German army would be in the field till the war was over. The Great War originally thought to be short now seemed to go on without end. The territory held by the Allies and Central powers had barely changed since the beginning of the war. Thousands of lives were lost for mere inches. Despite the deadlock, the German army was committed to winning, and morale, although weak, was still there. The ability to rotate troops to the rear helped tremendously. A place to escape the horrors of war if for only a brief time. They endured the horrors of war for their Kaiser and country but foremost they fought for their fellow brothers in arms beside them. The bonds soldiers form in times of great struggle form as strongly as those they have with kin, literally.

Franz dug his shovel into the rocky soil with a sharp *thwack!* His face was red from exertion. The new machine gun position was halfway dug out. Two recent recruits from his company, Private

Abelard and Brenner, young men who looked barely old enough to shave, labored with him. Keeping the soldiers occupied helped them to stay sharp. The noise of bombardment messed with natural sleep for the men, and they became so used to rounds firing they became oblivious to shells falling even if only a few yards away. They lived like vampires in reinforced concrete caves waiting for rest days in the rear. Franz called for a break.

The men sat cross-legged with their trench shovels across their laps inside the dugout. Sweat trickled down Franz's neck and back. His hair clung to his head underneath his helmet, locking in the heat, cooking his thoughts. He glimpsed the sky, watching the brilliantly white clouds move slowly against the blue. He noticed a peculiar-looking cloud. A single cloud stood out giving an image of a giant eagle with spread wings looking down upon the earth. With very little breeze the majestic bird stood there hovering up in the sky. *Is it a trick of the brain to see such a stunning formation or is it a heavenly sight the German Empire will prevail?* The eagle, once a medieval symbol of the Holy Roman Empire, was now a symbol for the Germans. Franz studied the image lost in thought. He raised his head.

A shot from a rifle cracked from the allied direction. Dirt splattered a few feet away from the sitting men. Franz and the privates moved quickly to a prone position. *Blasted sniper! Our darn heads must have been sticking out too much. You let your guard down here, you're going to meet your Maker.* He slowly peaked out of the hole looking for the shooter. It was almost impossible to pinpoint the sniper's location unless another shot was fired. He winked up at the Eagle. *Are you looking out for me?* he joked to himself. "Let's get back to work but keep your head low, otherwise the Doughboys will use it for target practice."

After the post was completed, Franz released the men back to their sergeants. He stayed alone to set the sights for the zone of fire. Franz climbed out of the post and into the trench. In a flash, a black and tan blur struck him. Not a powerful hit, more an unexpected surprise. It was a large German Shepherd with a black and tan coat, a strongly developed chest, and a long, curved tail. The dog was filthy. Its luxurious coat was now caked with dried mud. It wore a medical supply pack with a white stripe across it with a red cross marking it as one of the valuable mercy dogs serving alongside the soldiers at the front. It held no cap in its mouth signaling it was probably returning from a trip to No Man's Land. It stood panting.

"Hey, boy, what are you up to?" The dog tilted its head in response. Franz pulled out a Knackebrot ration, a tasteless rye cracker, from his shirt pocket. The dog came closer to Franz's outstretched hand and after a few sniffs grabbed the cracker and devoured it, licked its lips with its large pink tongue then looked up for more. Tail wagging side to side the dog reached up and nibbled on his sleeve in an attempt to get more. There was no resisting the begging and adorable, loving doggy eyes. Franz gave another cracker then another till he ran out. "Sorry, boy, don't have anymore. Off with yah. Be a good soldier and get back on duty." Franz bent down and petted the dog on the head. Looking at this dog reminded him of his beloved German Shepherd named Schwartz back home. The dog reached up and licked his face.

Franz now tried to ignore the dog. He knew it was best to leave him alone. It would return to its handlers especially when it became hungry. The dog continued to follow him with a steady gait, its fur that wasn't coated in dirt softened by the sunlight.

Franz returned to the concrete bunker he called home.

Han's tisked. "Look at that dog, he looks so pitiful. We should at least give him a bath. The poor guy is filthy."

Franz looked down at the dog. "You want a bath, soldier?" The dog cocked his head. "Alright, give him a bath then send him to the handlers' station."

The men found a large metal container used to hold an ammunition store; it was as large as a tub. They removed the ammunition carefully then filled the tub with water. The dog's pack was removed and he was lifted gently into the tub. The water would be cold, but the dog was a soldier and could rough it. The dog was scrubbed down with a bar of soap, then doused with buckets of water. The soaked dog shook its body in a twisting motion spraying water all over the men who volunteered to bathe him.

They had little with which to dry the dog. Franz dried him with an extra blanket. "He looks like a big, fluffy bear."

Hans raised an eyebrow. "This dog has no ID tag with a name. Must have broken off." He placed his fist to his chin pretending deep thought. "What should we call him?"

Franz thought to himself. *He's a little beggar.* "Let's call him Pauper."

"Ha, that will work," said Hans.

"Does anyone have anything better?" Franz looked around. "Good, Pauper it is."

The dog was fed dry meat from the men's rations with plenty of water then accompanied the men to an assigned work detail. The work detail, from First Company, was tasked to help lay additional concrete in the fortifications.

Just as they arrived at their location a young private approached them. The private's face had a dimpled chin, with dark hazel eyes that glinted as he cracked a smile. He stooped low and ran his fingers through Pauper's soft fur. "There you are, Bolzen. Wow, you're so fluffy. Whatcha been up to, buddy? I was looking for you. You're needed to send a message to the rear." Bolzen jumped up and licked his face.

Franz rubbed Bolzen's head. "Sorry about that, the men took a liking to him. I guess they miss their furry friends back home. He reminds me of my own dog named Schwartz."

The private noted Franz's rank. He clicked his heels and stood straight. "Private Schneider, sir."

Franz smiled. "At ease, private, that's a good-looking dog there. We cleaned him up and gave him some chow. I must warn you the men are kinda getting attached to him. That dog is just as entertaining to the men as if a beautiful woman was handing out gingerbread."

"Thank you for the bath. We're seldom able to get them in. These dogs are busy. They work without complaint. The best soldiers in the army if you ask me."

Franz raised his voice, speaking crisply. "Time to give him back. Bolzen has work to do as do we."

A few groans of protest were heard.

Private Schneider looked at the men's slumped shoulders. "Hey, no long faces. When Bolzen gets back from his mission, as a favor for the bath, I'll send him to you for some fun. He loves to play fetch."

The men lined up and gave a quick goodbye pet to their new furry friend.

The platoon spent hours working concrete into wooden frames. A nearby observation post with spyglass kept an eye on No Man's Land. Not a sound came from the Allies, only occasional and random sniper fire. No enemy movement, just the odor of mud and an occasional whiff of decay. It had been a few days since any attack.

With the work finished in the early evening, they returned to the billeting area to relax and entertain themselves—entertainment that, as often was the case, was limited to swapping stories about back home.

Hans nudged Franz. "Adoph would have loved that . . ."

The door opened. The men grew quiet as if a general had entered the barracks.

Franz grinned. "Hey, Bolzen. Although I must admit the name Pauper suits him more. I can't really see the Bolzen in you." (*Bolzen* means bolt in German.)

"Sorry, sir, he was gone longer than usual. Maybe he found a girlfriend along the way." He caressed Bolzen's scruffy neck. "I'll be back to pick him up in the morning. Have fun, Bolzen."

Under the glow of electric light, the men took turns tossing the ball to Bolzen. They played late into the night. After the play, the lights were turned off. Along with an exhausted Bolzen, the men that slept soundly. Only an occasional soldier called for guard duty stirred the chamber.

Bolzen broke the dark silence with loud barking. In the tight chamber, the barking echoed loud and deep. The chirping bark continued unrelentingly. Franz awoke startled. In a gruff voice, he hollered, "Go on, boys, to your posts. Let's go. Schnell! Schnell!" *If nothing is out there at least the drill will keep the men on their toes.* First Company scurried out of their bunker, like ants out of their hill, and took up defensive positions. The alarm was sounded and nearby companies took up their posts.

They did not wait long. With the first rays of morning light came an eruption of artillery fire. A mass of soldiers followed immediately after in an attempt to overwhelm the defense line in a wave of bodies. The specific attackers were easily recognizable by the turbans they wore. They were the Indian colonial regiment that served under the British. These fighters struck the greatest fear into the hearts of the Germans because of their tenacity. They poured forward like rain in a monsoon onto the German defenses. Their officers hollered, pointing with sharp sabers. The Indians bled as machine-gun fire cut through them like a mower through grass. With their courageous charge, the dead were going to pile up like stacks of firewood. Heedless to the casualties, the Indian wave advanced up to the barbed wire defenses. Sharp wire ripped through their clothes catching them and making them easy target practice. The Indians navigated through the wire by walking over the corpses, as a bridge.

Loud drumming of close mortar fire opened up on the attackers but still, they continued to advance. A dozen attackers managed to spill into the trench, shouting in a language the Germans did not understand, but their faces gave away intentions. They were prepared to fight to the death.

Franz unloaded his rifle into the enemy. After exhausting the clip he dropped his rifle. In a quick motion, he pulled out his pistol, his hands tight on the handle. *Pop, pop, pop,* until *click.* A grim-faced attacker aimed his rifle at Franz. Franz slumped his head in anticipation of the bullet. A bullet tore through the attacker instead.

"You were so close you nearly blocked my shots," said a fellow soldier in a grey uniform that moved to Franz's left side.

"*Traurig und Danke*," (sorry and thank you) Franz said.

"Don't mention it."

The Indians began to quickly fall. The last attacker riddled with bullets hurled something before he dropped.

"*Shite*" cussed the soldier by Franz's side.

With a metallic clink, a small canister fell in front of them. A pop sound followed by a hiss. The distinct scent of mustard was smelled.

Franz's face turned pale. "Get out of here! *Schnell!* Masks on!

The Germans scrambled for their lives. Franz grabbed the closest soldier and shoved him over the trench to safety. He followed closely behind, hoping his men followed his lead. Franz made sure the soldier he grabbed had his gas mask on then he placed his own on. He looked like an alien with two large lenses for eyes and a heavy canister that protruded from the mouth like a sack used to feed a horse.

Under a cloud of gas, oblivious to the danger, the Indians continued to strike. A dozen more dropped into the trench. They began to choke and gag. The poisonous gas worked its deadly magic, blistering the flesh and searing lungs. One attacker slowly moved like a zombie about to fall. His head jerked back with a rifle shot. A machine gun took up position and rained hail into them. None survived.

A deep-sounding horn bellowed retreat, for the battered Indian regiment. They fell back bravely, returning fire as they escaped. With the battle over, the Germans turned their full attention to assisting the wounded. With masks on, Germans ran to help their struggling brothers in arms. Those affected by the gas screeched and gasped for breath. It was a scene out of a horror movie. Mustard gas destroys by blistering the throat and lungs if inhaled in sufficient quantities.

Even those that put their mask on in time were affected if the gas soaked into their uniforms, producing horrible blisters all over the body. Anyone with contaminated uniforms had to be stripped of them as fast as possible. The uniforms then had to be washed.

Just after sunrise, the clean-up was completed and all the wounded were removed for medical care. Fran searched for Bolzen. *He may be a bundle of fur, a furry friend, but he's a soldier in my eyes, one that helped protect his brothers and deserves recognition.* Bolzen was found curled up near his handler Private Schneider.

"He looks exhausted," Franz said.

"He sure is. Out all day yesterday then back to play with your company. Probably was barking his head off all through the attack."

Franz went to one knee and petted the dog. "Bolzen alerted us before the attack. I don't know if the watch would have caught it. Who knows, another minute before taking the line and the attack may have succeeded and we wouldn't be standing here." He paused. "I have something for him."

Franz pulled out a worn sergeant rank patch from his pocket and pinned it to the medical backpack Bolzen carried. "This used to be mine. I think he's earned a promotion."

Franz clicked his heels then saluted Bolzen. Schneider did the same. Nearby soldiers that watched the impromptu ceremony saluted also.

"I hereby promote you to Sergeant for your quick action and dedication to your duty." He turned to Schneider. "Your right, Bolzen is a good name."

The Germans remained on high alert, waiting for an attack that never came. Instead of an attack, their enemy signaled for a cease-fire to collect the wounded and dead. A temporary truce was granted. The Germans watched as the allied medics, a force too small for their task, began to work. As a sign of respect, the German medics came out to assist them.

As Franz looked across No Man's Land, now at peace, he witnessed litters crisscrossing the field with wounded first then the dead. He placed his pipe in his mouth, imagining there was tobacco in it. He nodded in prayer. *Dear God, I am forever grateful for my survival, and pray for you to help those wounded, our boys as well as theirs.* The answer as to why God allowed war eluded Franz. *War, so evil. The suffering, the maiming, the dying.* The only answer he came up with was: *A man reaps what he sows. War, although horrific, is just another of man's sins. God commanded us not to kill. It's man's choice, not God's.*

CHAPTER 13

GONE IN A BLINK

Kitchens are the birthplace of heavenly aromas, the kind that can transport your memories to home. This kitchen that was deep underground was walled with grey wood and did not spark homey aromas nor fragrances necessary for that. An unpleasant odor of cooked meat filled the mess area just outside the kitchen door. 1st Company was lined up to receive their evening meal from pale-faced cooks that rarely glimpsed the sun. They feared to venture out and receive a bullet.

Franz motioned to Hans' plate. "So what animal do you think that came from?"

"Don't know but it sure smells good," Hans said sarcastically.

"It's from trench rats," the server winked.

Hans gave a look of disgust.

"I'm joking, it's sausage. Although it looks about to spoil. Here, big guy." He spooned an extra heaping scoop of boiled potatoes on Hans' plate. "Don't look so blue."

Hans and Franz made their way into the crowded and noisy dining area. They sat on two well-worn wooden chairs surrounding a table made from two stacked wooden crates with a rainbow of splinters that they tried to avoid touching.

Hans stabbed at the mystery meat with his fork then swallowed a bite.

"It actually isn't that bad, but definitely not how my mother used to make it."

"I bet it is a rat," smirked Franz.

"Ha!" Blurted Hans as he took another bite.

The battalion commander Colonel Schmidt entered, followed closely by a young lieutenant. The Colonel was a grizzled veteran of countless battles. A large puckered scar traced from his right eye across his nose to his left cheek. He radiated a "don't mess with me" attitude. The lieutenant's unblemished face with hints of youthful softness appeared a mirror opposite to the Colonel. His eyes held an air of innocence about him. He reminded Franz of the character Peter Pan. The two polar opposites stopped in front of Hans and Franz's table. Hans and Franz immediately stood up at the position of attention. The room previously filled with loud conversation quieted immediately.

"At ease, men. Please be seated," said the Colonel. Hans and Franz sat back down, Colonel Schmidt and Lieutenant remained standing. "Franz, good to see you. I've been meaning to give this to you." He placed a rank insignia patch on the table. "Two pips to replace your one. Sew this on your shoulder board. Congratulations, Captain."

Franz's face lit up with pride. "Th-thank you, sir."

Schmidt stretched for his hand and tapped the insignia. "No, it is I who must thank you. You have done a tremendous job leading 1st Company. The fatherland is grateful to have you." He motioned to the lieutenant. "I would like to introduce you to Lieutenant Gunter Meyer. He will be your new second in command. He's green but he's a quick learner. This is his first time to the front, I need you to get him quickly up to speed."

Franz shook Gunter's hand. "Welcome to 1st Company."

"The best darn company under the sun," said Hans.

Schmidt pulled out a pocket watch and glanced at the time. "Well, Lieutenant, I leave you in very capable hands. Listen to Franz, do what he says and you'll be fine."

The loud noise of conversation began the moment the Colonel departed.

"Please, Lieutenant, have a seat. Have you eaten yet?" Said, Franz

"No, sir."

"Hans?"

"On it."

Franz pulled over an extra chair while Hans collected a plate of food and a mug of beer then placed it in front of Gunter.

"Your first time at the front, " the Colonel says. "Have you seen any action yet, Lieutenant?"

"No, sir. Just came out of the training depot yesterday. You may be wondering why I'm here with your frontline unit. You see, my father pulled some strings. Let's just say my father is very connected. My favorite uncle said that if I ever made my way into the army to come and see him. My uncle is Sergeant Mueller. We grew up together, Mueller's only a few years older than me? His mother birthed him a few years before her daughter had a child. I figured instead of just a visit I would join him instead."

Franz raised an eyebrow. "Sergeant Mueller? Oh, Lukas. He's with his platoon on watch, freezing their tails off I bet. The wind is fierce today. They should rotate out and be here soon for chow."

Gunter picked up the sausage, gave it a deep whiff then turned his nose in disgust.

"The first rule of soldiering is to eat what is issued to you," Hans laughed. "Unless your like this guy and don't eat unclean meat."

Franz harrumphed. "It sometimes has its advantages."

After the meals were finished, the men waited for Lukas and his platoon to return from watch duty. The platoon entered, faces red from blasts of cool air, then lined up for food.

Although Lukas hadn't grown into his mustache yet he held wisdom in his eyes. Eyes that had witnessed the horrors of war and learned from them. These eyes now bulged at the sight of Gunter. "Well, I'll be a lindworm. Gunter! Oh my God. It's you." Lukas embraced Gunter. "Ah, never thought I'd see you here." Lukas released Gunter then frowned slightly. "Hey, aren't you too young to enlist? You were finishing school, weren't you?"

"Hey, I'm seventeen. School can wait. Father was fine with it. It was my mom who was difficult to convince. I pestered her until she couldn't stand it anymore. I can serve then finish school afterward. I don't want to miss my chance to serve and see some action. I hope there are a few Tommies left for me?"

Lukas let out a short sigh. "Honestly, I can't say you made the best decision, but you're here now." Lukas looked at Franz with determined eyes. "Sir, would you mind if I take charge of this Lieutenant and show him the ropes?"

Franz turned to Gunter, "By all means, Sergeant. Lieutenant, you're fresh from the training depot. You have a lot to quickly learn and unlearn. Pay attention to your uncle, he's been in the crap for a while now. He knows a thing or two."

Lukas grinned. "I have something for you." He noticed the new rank insignia on the table. "Captain." He handed a tattered, faded yellow envelope to Franz.

"What is this?"

"You'll see, open it up, I got it from Private Schneider. When I gave Bolzen back to him this morning, he told me that he and Bolzen were moving to a new post. He gave me this, said it's a goodbye present from Bolzen to you."

Franz unfolded the envelope gently, revealing shredded brown tobacco inside. "Outstanding!"

Franz pulled out his pipe, stuffed it with tobacco then lit it. Leaning back on his chair he puffed out smoke rings. The smoke pooled at the ceiling above him, then leaked through the cracks of the wood ceiling.

"Some skat, gentlemen," said Hans.

Hans produced a deck of cards and the game began.

Gunter tapped Lukas's shoulder. "Do you remember Leonie?"

"Yes, the one with the…."

"Yes, that's her. I married her before I shipped out."

"You sly dog, good for you."

"Father floated me a little money. We're already set up in a small apartment. I have a good job lined up at the patent office once school is done."

Franz raised an eyebrow. *You have a plan, kid. I just hope it works out for you.* Franz stood up. "Gonna check on the men and tuck them in. Remember, Gunter, listen to Lukas, I mean it. Also, remember an officer needs to set an example. Work beside the men and they will respect you. You'll be ok, son." *I hope so. I truly do.*

The next morning Lukas introduced Gunter to the men in his platoon then he took Gunter to take his first peek at No Man's Land. They stopped at a covered machine gun nest with a sheet metal roof, above that a few feet of dirt. Although it was daylight the room was dim, the only light coming in was from a three-foot by two-foot slit. This slit would be the only thing visible to any attackers. A four-man machine gun team was present.

Gunter pointed at the Maschinengewehr 08 machine gun. "How can the Tommies go against that?" He whistled. "It's a monster of a thing."

"It sure is a monster. This beast is operated based on a short barrel recoil and a toggle lock. Once cocked and fired the MG 08 continues firing rounds until the trigger is released. This baby kills at a distance of 2,200 yards. Go ahead and look out the trench periscope. If observers see anything they signal and the gun is manned."

Gunter ducked underneath the slit as he made his way to the scope. He looked through it. "Really isn't much to see. Some charred trees. Lots of holes and mud."

"What did you expect?"

"Not sure, maybe a little excitement."

"Some dancing girls?"

"I wish."

Gunter stood up straight with a wide grin on his face. He walked over to Lukas, towards the slit. He was in the center of it when the sound of a ping of metal was heard. Gunter slumped to the ground with a bullet through the side of his helmet. Bright red blood flowed from underneath his helmet.

"Sniper!" hollered a soldier in the nest.

"Gunter!" Lukas ran to the body. He removed the helmet and cradled Gunter's head in his hands "No, no!" He stared into Gunter's lifeless face then with bloody fingers closed Gunter's eyes. Lukas remained holding his nephew, his mind unable to comprehend what he witnessed. One of the soldiers present took up the machine gun and began to blast a few rounds towards where he thought the sniper was. It was an exercise in futility; the snipper was not located. The rounds ceased.

Franz barreled in then, quickly examined the scene. *"Shite."* He squeezed Lukas' shoulder tightly. "Come on, Lukas." He softened his voice. "You need to let him go."

With a glazed cast to his eyes, Lukas let go of Gunter. He stood up then walked out of the nest.

It was dark when Lukas staggered back towards his sleeping quarters. He spent the day walking the trenches searching for answers that did not come. He took solace in the common thought among soldiers *that if you were going to die in war, it's best to get it in the beginning than at the end of it.* Dying at the beginning you would at least be spared the suffering. It was not perfect solace for Lukas.

All hints of youthful softness were already gone, replaced with hard lines to his face. Another line was added.

A blur of black and tan fur ran toward him as he moved to his bunk. Bolzen looked up at Lukas as if he wanted something. *What, boy, I have no treats for you.* Bolzen followed him like glue as Lukas made his way to his bunk. He jumped on the bunk and attempted to curl up on top of Lukas. Lukas nudged him off. The dog attempted again and again with the same result. Lukas realized that he would not win the battle. He curled up in a fetal position leaving enough room for Bolzen. Bolzen jumped up and gently rested his head on the legs of Lukas. The serenity of sleep took them both.

CHAPTER 14

LIGHT THE DARKNESS

Germans fighting on the western front knew the Americans had recently arrived on French soil. The Americans, at first belligerent to be involved in European affairs, now would come in waves like a storm surge. Uncle Sam would bring his big stick. Germans had long feared American entry into the war, however, morale was high regardless of four years of bloody stalemate along the Western Front. Optimism came from recent success in Italy, Greece, Serbia, and especially Russia. The defeat of Russia following her rise into revolution freed up German divisions from the east to reinforce the western front. Everything was going perfectly for the German Empire at this point of the war. But to ensure the victory they needed to take into account the Americans. They began to plan decisive strikes along the Western front before millions of American soldiers along with British reserves throughout the British Empire appeared in battle. It was their best chance to end the showdown once and for all. It would be the perfect kill-or-be-killed situation.

1st company was rotated to the rear. This would be their final chance to recharge before the offensive named "The Kaiserschlacht" or "The Emperor's battle" began.

On arrival, Franz went immediately to the barracks for a shower to wash off the everyday filth of living at the front. He had just changed into a fresh uniform when Hans and Lukas approached him.

Franz placed his soft cap on. "Nothing like a fresh uniform. Even nicer with my new pips sewn on it."

Hans clicked his heels. "Captain, good news. After picking up the new replacements, the company is at full strength. I never thought I'd see the day. We will need a new platoon sergeant." He turned to Lukas. "Maybe one with a better-looking mustache this time."

"Ha, very funny," groaned Lukas. "Sir, the replacements are all veterans from the east. They won't need any babysitting. I've been talking with them. I thought we had it bad. You should hear the stories they tell about their fighting the Russkis."

Hans interrupted. "Some more good news. Our company has been invited to the Red Cross recreation building. The volunteers are putting on a movie sponsored by the Women's League. If we leave soon, we can make it in time before it starts. Not sure what movie they'll be showing, but it would be a nice escape for the men."

Lukas cast a blank stare. He spoke in a hoarse whisper, "A temporary escape. Give their eyes a different dance to see."

Franz patted Lukas on the shoulder. "A movie sounds good. I could use an escape myself. Get the men assembled that want to go then let's head over."

Half the company arrived just outside the Red Cross recreation building. Propaganda posters were plastered all over the building, covering every open space. One, in particular, caught Franz's attention as he walked into the building. The poster held an image of a burned village with the caption, "This is how it would look in German lands if the French reached the Rhine." Franz was proud that German soil remained relatively safe from widespread invasion. *All of our suffering at least protects our families from the horrors we have witnessed.*

Chairs were available, but not enough to seat the large crowd that entered. Those without a seat would get the floor in front of the chairs pressed closely beside one another. The air in the room held a whiff of a funky smell. It was obvious some men had not showered yet on their return to the rear. The projector ran on top of a rickety wood desk that should not have been standing. The title across the screen was "The Ballet Girl." The room was noisy and rowdy at times. The men watching would hoot and laugh at certain scenes. Nearly all of them it seemed.

It was a temptation to quiet the men but Franz enjoyed hearing his men laugh and his own. It was also nice to see women on the screen. It led him to the pangs of missing his wife and three daughters. He wondered what they would be doing at this moment while he enjoyed the silent picture show. *Erna would be in her sanctuary. Her kitchen. Maybe she would be churning butter. As much as I offer she never lets me touch the churn. Herta would be rehearsing with her cello. Emma and Anne would be giggling and dancing to the music. Old Schwartz would be curled up near the fireplace.* Franz's heart warmed with these pleasant thoughts. As quick as a heart can be warmed with pleasant thoughts, it can also be chilled by dark ones. It depends on what you are given, is it a bloom or is it a thorn?

As Franz departed the room, a red cross nurse blocked his exit. She wore a nun's adornment, a black dress, a white veil, a white apron, and a red cross armband. Her face was wrinkled with trenches and large frumpy cheeks that showed her age. She held a stoic expression on her face. "Excuse me, captain, is your name, Franz Fischer." Franz nodded. "My name is Sister Agnes. Franz, we have news from your family back home. Please come with me."

Franz followed. He tried to decipher the message from her face but it was unreadable. No sign of amusement or bliss reflected.

Franz's mind raced. *Would they find me to tell me good news? Probably not.*

A gentle touch on Franz's shoulder.

"Do you want me to stay?" Hans spoke with concern in his voice.

Franz turned to Hans then feigned a smile. "Thank you for the offer, Sergeant. I'm afraid I'll battle whatever this is alone. Keep the men out of trouble. They should be re-charged some. Make sure that extra energy doesn't get them into trouble. I'm sure I will not be that long."

Franz followed Agnes two blocks to an old stone cottage that appeared to have popped out from the pages of a Grimms' fairy tale. The building had short dirty windows deeply recessed into the stonework with monstrous amounts of bright green ivy clinging to it. A large, crude red cross was painted over the entrance. They walked into a spacious room filled with carts of wounded in various stages of recovery. Almost half the carts were full. Nuns continued on their tasks and only stopped to give a short nod to Franz and his guide. The pair made their way to the back of the building to a narrow wooden door in the back.

The door was opened revealing a room pitch black. A lit match by Agnes brought a sudden light to the dark. She lit a candle that illuminated a worn, paint-chipped four-by-two table. In the grains of the wood, there were streaks of cream color. The room was unfurnished except for two beat-up-looking stained wood chairs, one on each side of the table. The dim light flickered as it struggled to replace the darkness giving an eerie vibe to the room.

"Franz, I will not stall anymore. I'm afraid I do not have good news for you. The Red Cross received a telegram from your village in Westphalia a few days ago. We knew your company was rotating to the rear soon, so it was deemed proper to tell you the news in person instead of handing you a telegram." She cleared her throat. "Your daughter Emma has passed away from influenza." She let out a soft breath. "I'm sorry for your loss. I know it will be hard not being there with your family during this time of grief."

Franz's heart sunk. He squeezed his eyes shut as his right hand went over his mouth. His left hand clutched the table.

"Please have a seat," said Agnus.

Franz collapsed into the chair in front of the desk. Images of Emma, her curly hair bouncing as she danced in laughter, filled his mind. Then he imagined her coughing and suffering from the effects of influenza. Her death would not have been quick or kind. Anger took hold of his heart. He clenched his fist. *Why did I survive and she didn't? The Lord had plenty of chances to take me into his arms, instead, you take this perfect little girl.* Uncontrollable tears ran down his face.

Agnes's face, no longer stoic, now softened to an expression of sympathy. "God works in mysterious ways, we can not fathom to understand. But know that there is a plan. Take time to devote yourself to the Lord and the plans may be revealed." Her voice struggled as she held back a well of tears. "Grief has no expiration date, my son, but it should help to know that Emma is in the arms of Jesus."

"I'm a Jew," Franz retorted gruffly after a sniffle. He pulled out his star of David medallion and showed it to her.

Agnes' face looked clearly confused for a brief flash. "Ooh, so was Jesus. Your daughter is in the presence of the Almighty Father of us all. Christians or Jews, we have the same Father." She gently pulled Franz's hands together and cupped her own over them. "I will pray for you and your family."

At a loss for words, Franz muttered only two words, "Thank you."

Agnes lifted her hands. "May the blessings of God go with you, my son. The burden of grief is heavy. If you need to talk to someone I am here. Is there anything you would like to talk about? Perhaps a walk with me before you return to your men?"

Franz wiped his eyes with his hand. His expression feigned strength, but it did not fool Agnes. "I am grateful for the offer but I would like to be alone for a while."

"Very well then," Agnes handed Franz his telegram. "May mercy, peace, and love be multiplied to you."

Franz stuffed the telegram in his pocket then rose from the chair. Agnes escorted him to the exit of the building. Franz slowly made his way back to the barracks. His mind was a quagmire of emotions. He knew death wasn't kind. He had seen so much of it on the battlefield. He also knew he needed to keep his wits together for the sake of the men under his command. The winds of war were changing. A large German offensive would begin soon. Their lives depended on him. There was nothing he could do but move forward. He concluded he would mourn when his path returned him to his family and if he didn't survive the upcoming offensive he would join Emma in God's embrace. His mind may have thought this but his heart did not and it took on the weight of grief.

CHAPTER 15

MIRAGE OF VICTORY

Spring 1918, the German offensive commenced. It started with a barrage that included gas attacks plastered over an area of 150 square miles between Arras and La Fere France at the Western Front controlled by the British. The German plan was to concentrate and attack the British, not the French. It was determined by the German command that the British-held area was the weak link. It was thought British soldiers were forced to fight and so weary of sitting in the trenches that many cut their throats during leave, additionally if the order was not maintained, they would desert in droves. After the bombardment, the German plan was to quickly overwhelm the British defenses then destroy the enemy's command and communications centers. This quick victory they believed would restore mobility to the Western front and win the war for the Empire before the Americans made an impact. A gigantic attack force of over 58 divisions waited to move up the basin of the river Somme and lead the German Empire to victory. Victory, a long-forgotten dream was indeed possible, but nothing could go wrong.

Franz watched the largest artillery bombardment of the war shoulder to shoulder with First Company. The spectacle was Dante's inferno come to life. Explosions of dirt and debris erupted continuously on the enemy lines for hours. Just after the last shell fell an intense fog rolled over No Man's Land. A vast haze that swallowed craters, tree stumps, and corpses from view. No matter, the German officers had memorized their maps and orders. They were ready to end the war.

Franz waited in silence watching low clouds swallow objects upon the battle-torn earth and vanish around the soldiers. The silence grew deeper as Franz listened to the rhythm of his heartbeat waiting for a shrill whistle to blow, signaling the attack to start. Sweat dripped down Franz's back as he looked to the left and right of himself. He saw the faces of young men that had so much of life yet to be lived. *How many more will not return home to their families?*

A high-pitched whistle sound broke the silence followed by an echo of *"Aufladen!"* The German army came to life in a great tide of grey. With battle cries of *"Deutschane Uberalles!"* translated as "Germany for all!" the British were taken completely by surprise as the attackers smashed through their frontline defenses. They retreated as the Germans pressed hard to gain as much ground as they could. For years very little territory moved on both sides. Into, through, and over the trenches and wires, they laid out a feverish energy of destruction. In a short time, the advance pushed nearly forty miles. This was the largest advance of any side since the beginning of the war.

It had been years since First Company was able to move beyond No Man's Land. Franz kept a watchful eye on his men during the advance. A good shepherd that tried to keep his flock alive. He leaned on his three platoon sergeants for support. Company leadership needed to make smart decisions like not committing a frontal assault on a machine gun nest when you could go around to take it out. First Company's casualty numbers were light, that is until the British woke up.

Maybe the German command understood the attack well but not the logistics. Their army quickly drew low in critical supplies such as food and ammunition. Although stunned at first, the British now countered with accurate, deadly fire. They were well acquainted with every piece of land and they put that knowledge to good use. Choosing to attack the British instead of the French was a grievous mistake. British resolve was strong and their army was well supplied. They fought back viciously, making the Germans pay dearly for every inch they took. In hindsight, had the Germans attacked the exhausted, dispirited French, perhaps they would have folded?

First Company remained spread out as it advanced towards an occupied ridge about a quarter-mile away. They moved through a large field of green wheatgrass as tall as a man's waist. The grain moved as an Elysium-weaved blanket upon the earth, happy in its place. They stooped low trying to hide their movements as much as possible. Franz heard a pop followed by a whoosh from an oncoming mortar shell. He looked around for any cover, a pile of debris or rolled barbed wire or anything. Nothing but the tall grass for protection. Instinctively, he curled up in a fetal position clutching his helmet on his head. "Cover!" he sputtered to the men around him. Not enough warning. The shell fell, sending chunks of earth and two men hurling through the air. His vision framed by stalks of green, he watched in horror as two torn bodies fell back to the earth. The sound of rifle fire released from the ridge. The First Company returned fire against their enemy. Franz got up to one knee and returned fire with his rifle. With the smell of spent powder thick in the air, he calculated his situation.

Frans grabbed the closest soldier, a Private named Schindler. Schindler was well known for his nervous energy. "Go fetch Hans and tell him to collect the other platoon sergeants here. Be quick about it. We're in a dang bird hunt and we're the birds. Keep yourself low."

First Company's three platoon sergeants surrounded him. They all lay prone on the ground.

Hans spoke first. "We're hitting strong resistance. The Brits aren't crumpling like they're supposed to. If we keep advancing, our company won't be at full strength for long."

Lukas spoke next. "Getting low on ammo. We've collected everything we can from the dead and wounded, only a handful of grenades left and we'll have to make every bullet count. I fear we can run out of ammo," added Lukas.

Franz turned his attention to Finn, the newest platoon Sergeant. His chin was divided by a cleft, his nose crooked from a brawl when he was younger. He had a lifeless gaze as if he had seen too much blood. "What do you think of our situation, Finn?"

Finn cleared his throat. "I'm new at First, I don't have much to say. I agree with the other two."

Franz gave a dismissive puff. "I asked you, 'What do you think, sergeant?'"

Finn rolled his eyes, "Thinking that command made a mistake. We're going to get butchered here as sheep led to slaughter. We could lose half of us in this assault."

Franz digested Finn's words. "I agree the situation is dire." Franz exhaled, shaking his head side to side. "We should fight as good soldiers but we also have an obligation to do everything we can for those in our care to survive this war. I love my country and I'm willing to die for it, but not to just throw life away needlessly. Should we die for a victory that is not coming? This great advance has failed and it should be stopped. Command knows this but will not halt. I want you men to swear to me that we return as many men home to their families as we can. This must become our mission."

"I'm with you." Hans placed his strong, callused fingers on Franz's shoulder. "Whatever you think is right."

"We will not continue the attack on the ridge," Franz's voice wavered slightly. His hand slipped into his coat pocket and he squeezed his pipe.

"Agreed," Lukas and Finn spoke as one.

"The Tommies have the higher ground. We have no artillery support. I believe Finn is right, we will lose half of us. So we take the ridge, then what? We won't hold it long. Inevitably the Tommies will push us back. This ain't going to happen."

A shell exploded nearby, splattering dirt and grass clumps into the air. Franz absently brushed the dirt from his uniform and continued, "Second Company is to our left, and Fourth Company is to our right. They're just out of range to see us." Franz raised his arm in the air, the one with the stub for an index finger. "Hold your fire! Hold your fire!" The call for a ceasefire resounded. Franz pulled out a worn dirty rag from his pocket. "This isn't very white, I've tried to wash the bloodstains out of it. But it will have to do." Franz tied the cloth to the tip of his rifle. He hoisted up the flag. Firing on the ridge began to slow then stopped. Franz stood up.

"You think that's wise?" questioned Hans.

"Shhh."

Franz began to walk uphill. First Company witnessed Franz's bold move as he moved towards the ridge. A current of wheat stalks fought him until he cleared the field and made it to the top.

"Ok, Hun, not another step."

A rifle bolt pulled back. Franz froze. His heart raced and everything appeared in slow motion. A short British officer approached. He was several inches to a foot shorter than average. He had a large straight nose, determined chin, and blue-gray eyes beneath thin brows. The officer rank was Lieutenant but regardless of his low rank and size, he held an air of authority. Alongside the lieutenant stood a soldier of similar size with no rank markings.

"Thomas, translate for me. First time I've seen a white flag go up. Well, let's face it. It's not very white, is it?

Thomas translated quickly and in perfect German.

Franz smiled. "It's the best white I have on such short notice. The wind has changed, my friend. My ship is being steered by a different current. We're going to lose this fight. We can win today but not for long. Now understand, we do have sufficient arms and ammo to take this ridge. But we're not going to."

Thomas continued to translate to the Lieutenant.

"You're not?" delivered as one word by the Lieutenant.

"Yes, we're going to pull back just out of range. Keep shooting at us periodically. When our command gives us orders to retreat, we'll pull out and nobody dies. If we continue to fight each other, men dying won't be the greatest loss. The greatest loss if we continue is losing a part of us inside that knows that needless death could have been prevented."

"Don't jockey with me. I know something about that. So you'll simply pull back?"

"Yes."

"Alright then. His majesty's men will take that offer. We will shoot over your heads. And you better do the same. Get going. And, Jerry."

"Yes."

"See you soon."

"Not if I see you first, Tommie." Franz winked.

Franz returned to his men. First Company immediately pulled back. As they retreated, they returned fire aiming far above this ridge. To give the appearance of an advance they continued to a tree line then stopped just before entering the tree cover. They kept rifle fire going continuously back and forth with the ridge but sporadically to conserve ammo.

Thunder rumbled softly above as a messenger from the Fourth Company arrived. First Company orders were to pull back and dig in. Command deemed the advance on the British successful and wanted to lock in the gains before they prepped for a new offensive. *Lock in gains. Ach! We'll trench up here and never move again.* Franz ordered First Company to the safety of the woods far from enemy range and waited.

Was it a mutiny by First Company? The definition of mutiny is the forcible or passive resistance to lawful authority. Was the German command acting lawful, sending men carelessly to their death? A greater power was at play here. That of divine intention. Early graves were prevented by not following the orders of man to complete a near-suicide mission. Not a word was ever mentioned about First Company's failure to take the ridge, but memory and lessons would follow the men to the cemetery about what occurred.

The German spring advance was halted along with their chance to win the war before the Americans arrived. In August, the allies countered with an offensive called the second battle of the Somme. By September, the Germans had been forced back to their heavily fortified Hindenburg Line, built to replace the old front line as a precaution against a defeat.

CHAPTER 16

TRIAL BY FIRE

Octber 1918, American troops were receiving their baptism of fire in a short gap between No Man's Land. They were less than a quarter-mile from German defensive positions. Uncle Sam was receiving a bloody nose. The doughboys were quickly learning it would not be a simple walk in the park and battles were more fun in a book than in person. After an unsuccessful raid, they hurried back to their own defensive position. Heavy machine-gun fire zipped them down as they ran like a scythe cutting through wild oats. In addition to the bullets spraying the field, trench mortars rained fire from above. Soldiers not fast enough were shoved aside, one man was accidentally tripped and fell. They did not slow a step as their boots trampled him.

A shell blast hit near private Myles Archambault. He froze as his eardrums rang painfully. He staggered a few steps then fell to his knees. The pain continued as he tore off his helmet and held his ears. Tiny driblets of red leaked out of his ear. *I need to move. I'm a sitting duck.* He knelt covered in sweat, grime, and filth. His right hand sunk in the mud as he struggled to lift himself up.

Sergeant Lance Perkins, seeing Myles in distress, ran towards him oblivious of any danger. "You ok, Myles? You hit?" Lance shoved Myles's helmet back on then began to pat Myles looking for an entrance or exit wound. Myles, still stunned and partially deaf, could only shake his head left to right. "Let's get you the heck out of this flim-flam. Old Fritz has spied us out for sausages."

Lance half-towed Myles back towards the American line with a grip of iron. Vicious varieties of mud weighed down their feet, not making it easy. As they came closer to the safety of the American defenses, brave soldiers came out of cover to help. Myles was carried over the wire laced over a five-foot sandbag wall then lowered down to the ground. Medics immediately descended on him. His wound was not critical and they placed him on a stretcher to wait while they tended those more critical. He was able to watch the remaining battered Americans return with a spyglass that looked through the wall of sandbags.

Myles witnessed Lance hurl himself over the wire then run to help a hurt soldier struggling about fifty feet away. The wounded soldier, bloodied from many bullet wounds, stumbled forward like a zombie. It was like a scene out of a silent picture as he watched the episode unfold. Lance twisted his ankle almost immediately when he landed but took the pain with only a slight limp and grimace noticeable. Lance did not stop. The wounded soldier took a bullet to his back with Lance halfway to him. This final bullet ended his struggle for life. He fell like a sack of potatoes.

Lance, knowing his rescue effort was now useless, headed back towards the safety of the American lines. A *zip-zip* sound. Lance was hit in the back of his arm and leg almost simultaneously. He crumpled to the ground and cried out in agony. "Son of a gun. Stings like a F*****!"

Lance began to crawl back but he was not going anywhere soon. In what seemed like hours but in reality, was only a few minutes, he struggled through the muck that carried the stench of death and decay. Scarlet blood clung to his uniform as he dragged himself closer to safety.

Myles knew it was insane to attempt a rescue under a constant hail of bullets, but his heart began to pump rapidly for it. Adrenalin quickly washed away any shell shock remaining. He moved off the litter and looked over the parapet, hand squeezing the top of a sandbag. Lance had risked his life to save Myles and Myles wanted to return the favor. He became angry at first, a quiet, simmering rage that clenched his jaw. Temper turned into action, and he began to lift himself, prepared to jump over the wire but he was quickly held by nearby soldiers. "He saved my life! Let me go!" Myles's mouth snapped shut, and he turned his head to glare at the men holding him, daring them to speak otherwise.

Charlie, Myle's friend since basic training, approached. He shot Myles with an indignant look. "Come on, man, it's suicide if you go over the top. The Jerry's will shoot a volley into you faster than you can say dance."

"Would you look out there!" one of the soldiers holding Myles said.

Everyone turned to look at No Man's Land. Those holding onto Myles released their hold.

Charlie's jaw dropped. "Dear Mary and Joseph, would you look at that? Those snakes in the grass."

Three Germans with painted helmets in a disruptive pattern of green and tan crouched low, moving across No Man's Land towards Lance. They moved in a manner that displayed obvious training. The Americans concentrated fire on them but they could not hit the stealthy targets. Lance was hunted like a wounded deer. The Germans about twenty feet from Lance stopped their approach and aimed behind a tree stump at their target. A single shot rang out. Lance gurgled, "Mother," as he drew his last breath. The Germans had killed their prey then immediately moved back towards the safety of their defenses.

Myles's brain seared with anger. His mind sparked a white light that blinded him with rage. His natural senses disappeared and he became a wild animal. He spitted out every profanity he ever heard as he rushed over the wall heedlessly, over the barbed wire that caught then torn flesh and uniform.

The Germans focused on their return and did not notice Myles racing towards them. Bullets from the enemy lines ignored him as well. The hunters had now become the prey. There was no stealth in Myles's pursuit. One German glimpsed Myles and turned to shoot the mad man. The German's rifle jammed and Myles closed the distance as that soldier now dropped his rifle and drew his pistol from his side. With one blow of his fist, Myles dropped the man. Myles struck him again with his fist and then with the end of his rifle. Myles then moved to engage the two remaining Germans, who now charged towards him with bayonets sticking from their rifles. Myles moved his hip barely escaping a stick to his belly. With his left fist, he smashed the stabber's helmet. That German was temporarily stunned. The other attacker advanced. Myles reared back with the butt of his rifle and managed to deflect a stab to his throat by a mere breadth of an inch. He used the butt of his weapon to strike this attacker in the head. The force was strong enough to dent the helmet. The soldier went down. The first attacker jumped on his back. Myles bent low and tried to wrestle him off his back. In the struggle, Myles grabbed his opponent's knife from his belt and stabbed him under the chin straight up. A river of blood flowed from the wound. He returned to the other German still unconscious and slit his throat.

Myles sank to one knee clenching his fists all swollen, bloodied, and skin-torn. Rage suppressed into a single tear that rolled from his eye. He breathed deeply as he came back from his temporary lapse of sanity.

Shots returned from the German line hitting the ground close to Myles. Myles dove for cover behind a burnt-out tree stump. The char blackened his hand like his spirit. *So this is how it ends? As a dead man stuck in No Man's Land. The Huns will probably hunt me at night.* The incessant clamor of gunfire trying to pick him offbeat a headache into his skull. He looked back towards the safety of the American line. With his adrenaline faded, he thirsted. He reached for his canteen and took a big gulp. He coughed, spitting water over himself. As he placed the canteen back he noticed the sky become darker as a passing cloud blocked the sunlight. He watched the cloud pass. He thought his eyes played a trick on him: Just before the cloud completed passing by the sun he glimpsed a shining figure looking down.

Myles knew his only chance was to make his way back towards the American line. The Americans had just suffered a crushing defeat and they would not be advancing anytime soon. Just before the cover of darkness came, he began to snake on his belly back to his line. He slid behind a dirt pile thinking it was sufficient cover in the dimming light. He thought wrong. One bullet hit his helmet and another his foot near simultaneously. His face hit the dirt. Blood ran from his nose as he turned on his back then pulled off his helmet to look at it. *No bullet hole, only a headache. Not so lucky with my friggin' foot.* Blood poured from his boot. He tested a little pressure on the wounded foot. A stabbing pain radiated from his foot up his spine. Gingerly he removed his boot. Flashes of pain threatened to consume him. From his first aid kit, he pulled a long cotton Carlisle bandage and wrapped it tightly around the wound. As he did he groaned in pain, before he blacked out.

The Americans and Germans continued to trade shots back and forth. Both sides knew he was there. It was too dangerous for a rescue or a hunt. Myles was up shite's creek without a paddle.

Myles woke. Although he could not see in the darkness he pulled out his Bible from his shirt pocket. In an attempt to distract his mind from his throbbing foot he thumbed through the photos of his loved ones tucked inside. The act summoned up memories of his loved ones. It temporarily held back the tide of pain, but it was impossible to stop the waves from crashing. Without help, he would sink into the grave.

Franz listened to the sound of sporadic moans for hours coming from No Man's Land. The anguished cries tormented his heart. Without help, the American soldier would pass from this earth alone with only the angel of death to greet him at his end. *No soldier, no matter what side he fights on, should suffer alone.* His mind filled with peace as he formulated a plan to give first aid and small comfort to the miserable soul out there.

In the dead of night with only the moonlight to guide, Franz went over the top. He stepped lightly trying not to make a sound as he slowly made his way to the location where he heard the wounded soldier. Pulling the small metal cord on his "Dynamo" flashlight, which hung around his neck, he placed his hands over the lens tightly, letting enough light escape to see his target. A young stocky soldier lay there motionless. His heart gripped with concern as he moved closer. He showed his light on the body. *Shoot, is he dead already?* The soldier's chest rose and fell steadily. *Poor boy must have fallen asleep overcome with exhaustion.* The soldier clutched a stack of small photos in his hand. Franz placed his hand over the soldier's mouth. The boy immediately stirred, dropping the photos. Franz gripped the boy's mouth tighter with his hand. "Shhh. Hello," Franz spoke in an English word he remembered. He put a finger to his lips and gave another. "Shhh." The boy froze.

Franz quickly examined the soldier's body looking for any wounds to plug. The soldier had a large ding on his helmet with a tiny hole at the center, but miraculously he had no sign of a head injury. The injury that caused the moans was obvious. One foot was wrapped in a dirty blood-soaked bandage. *Perhaps the foot shattered with the impact of the round. The boy can't just simply hop up; he'll be picked off easily and the distance is too far for him to crawl back in this condition.* Franz removed a clean bandage from his pocket and wrapped it around the foot. He wished for something or anything to help the soldier's pain.

Maybe some whiskey if I had any? What more can I do? What I really need to do is get the boy back to his side of the line. I can drag him as far as I can and pray I don't get shot doing it. Darn it, my men need me. I can't risk it. Sorry, boy.

Franz watched the soldier carefully place his photos into the pages of a pocket-size Bible then place the book into his pocket. Franz sighed as he resigned to leave at that moment.

The soldier reached out and placed both his hands on Franz's right hand. "Thank You."

It was one of the few English words that Franz recognized. Franz pointed at his chest. "Franz."

The soldier pointed to himself. "Myles."

With a shake of his head, Franz abandoned his decision to leave the boy. He resolved to follow his moral compass and get the boy back, even at the risk of his own life. Franz bowed his head whispering in prayer, *Dear God, please protect me and not let the Americans spot me. They will shoot first then ask questions later. And give me the strength I will need to get him to safety. We are both in your embrace. Let your will be done.*

A flash of lightning stretched across the sky like a flame-filled dragon, lighting up the clouds. Followed quickly by the sound of thunder.

With Myles kicking off on his uninjured foot, Franz helped drag Myles towards the American line. Franz suffered pain in his lower back as he bent low in movement. He dealt with his sweat rising the same way a knight embraces his armor. Approximately thirty feet, as close as he dared to the American line, he stopped. After a gentle finger poke to Myles's forehead, Franz pointed to the American line then gestured with his fingers he was leaving. Myles understood he could not call out for help till Franz was safely away.

Franz carefully made his way back to the German lines. Myles, while waiting to be able to call out for help, drowsy from exertion, dozed off.

Franz made it back just before the first crack of dawn. On arrival, he sent a prayer to the heavens that the American soldier, his enemy, would be ok.

Myles woke up face down with a hard rain hitting him. His helmet was missing and the steady drops soaked his hair and clothing. Within a few minutes, he looked like he had been tossed in a swimming pool. He looked up to determine his bearing. He remembered where Franz pointed to the American line. He spotted barbed wire then called out with a scratchy, barely audible voice for help.

A reply came to his call. The sound of a rifle bolt pulled back. "Apple," a voice called out a challenge.

Myles quickly returned the password. "Pie."

"We won't shoot, keep crawling, yah doughboy."

A portion of wire moved away. Myles wormed his way through the mud and clasped a hand sticking out of the trench. He was dragged in and medics descended on him.

Myles was severely wounded yet still alive. Without the aid of his enemy, he surely would have perished. It was unknown to him why Franz saved his life. A puzzle he could not solve. The angel of death missed the path to claim his soul. For a human soul, due to free will, there are many paths to choose from. Franz chose the path that called to him. This path made him feel truly and deeply alive. This particular path pleases the Creator above all others, with a clear sign posted for those that look for it. The sign that reads *Love thy neighbor*.

CHAPTER 17

HIDDEN ANGEL

O ver the desolate battlefield, the wind blew. On the field, corpses lay exposed upon the charred and devastated landscape. If the wind remembers what it has witnessed, what would it say? Would the wind cry for the life that had once lived and is now dead? No, the wind simply blew over the carnage, but something did listen. Something that began before the wind ever blew. The wellspring of all that has always been. The Alpha and the Omega. The I Am. It heard the cries of the wind and a plan was already in progress.

A beam of bright light cast from the heavens onto the earth, specifically over the war scars of Europe. The beam was hidden from mortal eyes, but it was there. Out of the beam, an angel appeared to step onto the earth. The angel resembled a flawless image of a man. No earthly elements touched this heavenly being as it walked slowly, observing everything. As he observed he pondered. *Will the sons of Adam ever learn? They have been removed from Paradise, yet there are gifts that remain. The precious gift of free will. Will you use it to walk the right path? If you walk the right path, it will lead you back to Paradise.*

Hidden from man, the angel walked the ground seeing and discerning. It heard their prayers to heaven. It bore witness to the pain and suffering of men at war. It had witnessed warfare before but sensed this time it was different. Never till this time had man seen the horrors of war like this. Death on an industrial scale. *Maybe this will be a turning point for man. Maybe this time they will do something about it?* Men had only been in existence for a blink compared to eternity, but they were capable of learning even if they did not always listen.

Then it happened. The angel witnessed the act and prayers of a soldier loving thy enemy, thy neighbor. It smiled. *Maybe this is not the war to end all wars but a beginning to the end of them.*

The beam returned to collect the angel. The angel, a trusted messenger, would deliver its report.

CHAPTER 18

WOUNDED WARRIOR

Myles was placed on a stretcher then taken immediately to a khaki-colored tent with a red cross stitched above the entrance. This aid station at the front was used primarily for urgent care and triage but was severely limited beyond that. Medics cleaned Myles's foot and a doctor evaluated the messy wound. The doctor told Myles he was confident the foot could be saved but the wound needed proper care. He gave medics instructions to wrap the wound then take Myles directly to a field hospital with more resources to treat the wound.

A horse-drawn ambulance transported Myles to the closest field hospital. Sleep called and his eyelids grew heavy, but the bumpy ride prevented any winks. He winced in agony with every bounce and jolt of the rickety ambulance.

He arrived at the field hospital as a hollow shell completely drained physically and mentally. There was a horrible smell disseminating inside the entrance, that of a butcher shop. He was left alone on a cart waiting for the medical staff to collect and treat him. The aching of his foot ebbed and flowed like a warm tide, with waves of nausea adding to his torment. One of his saviors, a medic, came with a needle that stung like a wasp. He was stabbed with morphine. In mere seconds the morphine clouded his head and removed the pain. Spent from his ordeal, his eyes shut. While he slept his foot was operated on then stitched up. He was taken to a recovery area.

Myles came too slowly. He glanced around the recovery room. Wounded warriors filled both sides of the long rectangular tent spaced 3 feet apart. A soldier, thin with his skin sunken in a lifeless complexion, lay in a cart to his right. A thick bandage was wrapped around his neck. The cart to his left was empty.

He felt a piercing pain as he wiggled the toes of his injured foot. Panic filled his brain as he feared the pain was a phantom ache. He heard talk about feeling this pain once a limb was removed. Before he uncovered the blanket he said a quick prayer. *Dear Lord, I know that you love me and you are capable of anything. I know I have not been much of a praying man, I promise to pray more. Please let my foot be there.* He tore off the blanket then raised his injured leg. His foot was still attached. *Thank you, God!* His foot was heavily wrapped in blood-stained bandages but it was there. A wave of warmth passed through him. A feeling of inner peace touched his soul deep inside. He lay there on his bed still in pain but with a slight smile on his face.

That smile did not last long. Once the morphine effect was out of his system, throbbing began to appear in his foot. The throbbing felt like being repeatedly stabbed with a sharp needle. With an attempt to sit up he quickly realized how futile it was. The pain was too much to overcome. He let out a soft low moan. His head slumped in defeat.

"Do you want me to call for you?" A croaky voice called from the cart to his right. Myles raised his hand in an attempt to get his attention. The voice choked out, "Nurse!"

A nurse appeared quickly beside Myles's cart. Her face took his breath away. It was captivating accompanied by deep blue eyes and a flawless face. She wore a pale grayish-blue dress with a blood-stained white apron that covered her slim body just above her ankles. A red cross was centered in the top half of her apron. Her auburn hair was tied up in a thin white bonnet. She gently touched his arm. The touch caused a shiver to run down his spine. *I have a girlfriend but it's ok to look, isn't it?*

She spoke in a pristine, quaint King's English accent "I know you're in pain, mate, but I would rather not give you more morphine if I can prevent it. You are just out of surgery. I'm sure you are aware you had a nasty wound to your foot. It has been cleaned, stitched, and dosed in the orange powder of acriflavine to help keep it from infection. We need to keep a sharp eye on it. Don't want gangrene to seep in." She gave a warm smile. "I do have some medication I can give you for the pain as an alternative. Rum." She poured golden liquid from a white porcelain pitcher into a small tin mug. "Here." She handed Myles the cup. Myles gulped down the drink. The alcohol warmed and tickled his throat. He choked, causing spittle to roll down his chin. She gently patted his back between his shoulder blades then wiped the spittle with a cloth.

She gently lifted Myles to a sitting position, stuffing two pillows behind his back. The movement caused a wave of pain in his foot.

Myles ground his teeth. "What's your name?"

"Cybil." She poured another cup and handed it to Myles. "You need to sip this slowly."

"I think I learned my lesson," Myles said.

"I'll check on you in a little while," Cybil said. Cybil departed.

The cup of rum did little for pain but took the edge off, enough for Myles to fall back asleep.

A gentle voice woke him. "It's time to eat."

Myles looked up with his head in a fog, he massaged his temples. "Oh, hi, Cybil."

"I brought you some food, as you Americans would call it 'chow." She smiled then handed Myles a tin bowl filled with a dark brownish custard with a spoon sticking out of it.

He looked at it strangely. "What is it?"

"Beef tea custard. Don't give me that face. It's actually rather good." Myles harrumphed.

"Well, it was that or the calf's foot jelly," she laughed. I have more food to pass out but I'll return with some tea." Myles sniffed the bowl. His spoon swirled the ugly-looking color a few times. *Here goes. Sure hope it tastes better than it looks.* It did. The large quantity of sugar added gave it a pleasant sweetness. The bowl was emptied and licked clean.

Cybil returned. "Fancy a cuppa?" She said as she poured a cup of warm tea into a blue porcelain cup, one for him and one for herself. She took a seat on the empty cart next to him.

"How's the pain?"

"The wound still throbs something fierce but it's not as bad as earlier. I could use a little more rum."

Cybil took a sip of tea. "Well, I don't have any more rum for you, but I have these." She pulled out two shortbread biscuits from a pocket on her dress. She reached over and handed him one. "This you should enjoy."

"Thank you," Myles said.

Myles devoured his biscuit and Cybil delicately nibbled hers until finished.

Well, I wish I could say, 'How are you enjoying your stay?'" Cybil said. "You must be homesick. I know I am. A little disruption at home when I left, well, to tell the truth, I practically escaped. My family was rather not chuffed to bits with my decision to join the Red Cross and volunteer, but to their shock, I insisted. I imagine they are beginning to get over it now. I know they love me, that they are only looking out for me, but they can be stifling. What's the point of life if you can't really live the life you want?"

"I agree. My girl wasn't so keen on me enlisting in the army but I needed to do it. I could not live with myself knowing I did not serve when my country needed me."

"Your girl. Oh, your sweetheart. Well, I figured a man as lovely as you had someone back at home."

Myles's face turned a brief shade of red. He glanced away to quickly change the subject.

"I can see families getting upset with their sons joining the army. We risk life and limb but volunteering as a nurse, why would they balk at that."

"Well, my family is rather old-fashioned. They're holding on to an age that doesn't really exist anymore. They don't understand that the world has changed. You men sacrifice for the war effort, and women must do their part also. The last I heard from my family they were traveling to the States. They are staying in Newport, Rhode Island, at one of their summer homes until the war is over."

Myles's face lit up with surprise. "Newport. Well, that's not far from where I live. I'm from the state of Rhode Island. I live in Providence."

"Do you now? What are the odds? When I travel back there we must enjoy some tea together. Did you enjoy the tea I brought you?"

Myles realized he hadn't tasted a drop yet. He took a sip. It tasted disgusting. He feigned a smile. "Delicious." He drew out the word and she knew he didn't believe it.

"Truly, I caught your eyes. Earl Grey is. . . ."

A sound of a voice clearing from behind Cybil. A grey-haired motherly-faced pudgy nurse appeared, her arms folded. Cybil looked startled like a child caught in a cookie jar. "Joline. Sorry, I lost track of time." She turned to Myles, speaking quickly, "Well, I need to be going."

Cybil and Joline exited the room.

Myles' neighbor spoke in a voice that sounded like a frog, "What a beauty. I wish I could whistle. We haven't been introduced. I'm Tony. Oh, I see the look on your face. I know I sound funny. You see. Shot in the neck. I may talk funny for the rest of my life but at least I'm alive. We were getting it bad when the Huns dropped on us. We gave as good as we got, but most of my squad didn't make it."

Myles looked at Tony. *Poor guy.* Myles frowned. "Sorry to hear."

"Thanks. At least the boys aren't suffering anymore. I like to think they're laughing and drinking together in a pub in the sky."

Tony continued. "That nurse is a pretty one, ain't she? She's like a princess cut from a fairy tale. Every guy here has been trying to catch her eye. Never seen her sit down and have a conversation with anyone, although I haven't been here long, maybe a week or so, not really sure. I lose track of time. Most of us will be picked up from here and brought back deep behind the lines to a real hospital, complete with walls to recover. They didn't have room on the last trip for me. I'm sure I'll be on the next ride out." Tony went into a coughing fit.

"Do you want me to call a nurse?" Myles said with a hint of concern in his voice.

"I'm good," Tony forced out the words. The fit subsided. Tony grinned. "Hey, Romeo. I have a joke for you. The Germans have an arrangement. Since practically all Frenchies are named Pierre, a German would holler, 'Hello, Pierre!' An unfortunate Pierre would pop his head up with 'Oui?' and a German expert sharpshooter would place a slug into his temple. A lot of Frenchies died with 'Hello Pierre!' 'Oui?' 'Boom!' The Frenchie command stuck their heads together. 'This is nuts! Our men are kicking the bucket like flies.' At some point, the French chose to reciprocate the German plan. One of them hollers, 'Allo, Fritz!' No answer. 'Fritz!' Nothing. 'Hello, Fritz!' 'Is that you, Pierre?' 'Oui!' Boom!'"

It took a moment for the joke to sink in but when it did Myles laughed. Followed by Tony's croaky laughter. Laughter made Myles's entire body shake. Although the shaking drew searing pain, the laughter proved a good medicine that lifted both men's spirits. The medicine continued as Myles and Tony swapped every joke they knew back and forth. The other wounded laying on their carts, even those that did not hear the jokes, escaped in the sound to a better mood.

After the laughter ended Myles waited for the lights to be turned off. Blazing waves of pain rippled through his foot. Myles wished for morphine, rum, anything to numb the pain. He was about to yell for a nurse when a post carrier entered. The letter handed to Myles was enough to temporarily mask the pain.

Myles's unit had tipped off the postmen to his location. The letter was from Kathy. At first, letters came frequently from Kathy about one every week, which quickly changed to every two weeks, then they slowed to about once a month. In contrast, Myles religiously wrote to her weekly, pouring out his emotions and experiences at the western front. *I'd rather be holding you now than this letter. It feels like forever since our last embrace.* He pulled out his picture of her as he read the letter.

Dear Myles,

I just received your last letter. So the French are fed fresh bread and wine with their rations, how rather unfair that seems. I imagine if you take a Frenchman's bread away they probably wouldn't fight. Haha. Sounds like you had a ball at the YMCA concert in the rear. I'm glad the small band and singers were able to provide such good entertainment so far from home. It's great that so many have volunteered to come over to help lift morale. No concerts for me. It's been very boring over here.

I understand you want my help collecting some books for your unit at the front. You probably don't want to read my old copy of "Pride and Prejudice." I'm not the most organized. I will let your folks know about your request. I went for a marvelous hike with some friends, around Roger Williams Park. We thought we lost George but he turned up and set off his booby trap, giving us all a good fright from behind a tree. It was quite funny. To think he couldn't enlist because he is missing some toes. Well, gotta run. My sisters of course say hi. Miss you. Toodles!

Kathy

The breath that came from Myles was long. His shoulders sagged. He looked at Kathy's picture. He couldn't help but feel disappointed in the letter. *If she's so bored maybe she could write more. It shouldn't be that hard to collect some books to send. Well, she's in her world and I'm in mine. We're both living in our own bubble right now. Everything will be back to normal when I come home.*

After lights out, Myles struggled to fall asleep. In this dark place, no one could see him wince in pain. He swam in an ocean of unknowable depths of pain. He had to bite down on his lip to prevent himself from calling out. He pulled out his Bible and gripped it tightly. *Please, Lord, take away this pain and give me a peaceful night of sleep. I know you can help this pain wash away. I will do anything you ask! Wait! Am I praying correctly? You don't just barter with the Creator, it's not a tit-for-tat relationship. Sometimes pain brings us closer to God. And being close to God is a gift unto itself.* A long yawn. *If that's the case I couldn't be any closer to him.*

CHAPTER 19

FEVERISH DREAM

In a dream, Myles sat under an apple tree with his grandfather Everett. The branches spread out revealed rosy-colored apples. They both held a freshly picked apple. Myles curled his toes into the thick green grass. He crunched a bite of the juicy apple. Everett raised his eyebrow, a sign he would tell another of his long tales. Myles rolled his eyes.

"Myles, I see that look. No story today but I wanted to give you some advice. You're growing into a man. A young bird about to leave the nest. Remember not to soar so high. Well, I guess I could share with you a short story after all." Everett smiled. The story was familiar to Myles and one that his grandfather shared many times. "In order to escape imprisonment, Daedalus, a craftsman, gave himself and his son wings made of wax and feathers. He warned his son Icarus not to fly so close to the sun because the wax would melt. The fool Icarus didn't listen and fell to the earth when his wings broke off. Now maybe Daedalus was partially at fault. His son was young. Wisdom takes time to grow. Kinda like an apple tree. It takes years to bear fruit that can be harvested. Think before you jump. Do you understand?"

"Sure Gra—"

Myles woke. Sweat beads covered his face and forehead. His pillow, his undershirt, and pants were soaked in perspiration. His body temperature had risen with fever set in. The fever was working hard to battle infection.

With dry and cracked lips, Myles creaked, "Wa—Water." He groaned. "W-Water."

A croak from Tony on the cart next to him. "Nurse!"

Cybil handed Myles a tin cup filled with water. "Sip it."

Myles swallowed the water slowly. The warm water felt refreshing as it soothed his parched throat. Cybil dipped a white cloth in a pitcher of water then began to pat his face and forehead with it. "You poor soul. You're burning up something fierce. I'm getting the doctor." She saturated the cloth, folded it, placed it on his forehead then walked off to fetch a doctor.

Waiting for Cybil to return, the fever grew worse. Myles's body began to shiver uncontrollably. He looked both left and right and began to see cartoon characters from his favorite comic strip float around the room. Delirious, his heart pounded rapidly and his head ached with the pulsing of blood drubbing his skull. He passed out.

Another dream. Myles hovered over a battlefield high in the air, like a bird he soared. He looked down and viewed the scorched and pockmarked battlefield. Grey and black puffs of smoke drifted from the ruins into the sky. He drifted down to the outskirts of a small town. Lower and lower until he could read the town sign with the name "Bethune."

He landed softly on his feet in front of a house that had just finished burning. The roof was completely missing and ashen grey timbers were still smoldering. His mind tingled, as he fought to control the physical actions of his body. Unable to seize control, his body was moved by an unknown force. No panic or fear took hold, only a sense of peace. He glimpsed his clothing. He wore a stunningly bright white robe with sandals.

His body walked around the blackened home leisurely. Then it walked through a hollow entrance that once held a door. In front of Myles stood a perfect-looking man who seemed chiseled out of the finest marble. The man's skin was pale and flawless. His hair was brilliantly blond with eyes of the deepest blue. He was dressed in the same clothing as Myles.

The angelic man said, "Hello, my brother. I look forward to hearing your report. So many prayers lifted to heaven from the children of this world we are compelled to take note."

Myles's felt his lips move beyond his control. "This son of Adam I have observed has shown me much," the angel said, "just as the men before him. I view his soul to see this world from humanity's perspective. I see what is in their hearts. They are such sinners. They know the laws to follow, the ten most important are etched in stone, but they often ignore them to do their own will, not the Father's. The gift of free will is both a blessing and a curse to them.

"They have free will but occasionally the sheep need a shepherd to guide them to greener pastures. When warranted, and always out of love, we occasionally intervene to fulfill the covenant with them. To show the path of love so that they can be saved."

The dream shifted. Only perpetual blackness was seen. The darkness that swallows everything. Then there was light. At first, a solitary candle glowed holding back the darkness. Then another candlelight showed. Then another until the light was so bright that any living thing with eyes would have been blinded by its glory.

Cybil sat on a rickety wooden chair next to Myles's cart. She dabbed his forehead again with a wet cloth. You would have thought Myles's face with eyes shut would have looked stricken or in pain but it held a look of peace.

The doctor diagnosed Myles with trench fever. The most likely source of this fever, it was believed at that time, was a blood-sucking louse or shared living with rats. The initial treatment for trench fever was quinine, also used to treat Malaria, but it proved not effective.

The only treatment now was to keep the stricken comfortable and watch them ride out the fever with the hope they would survive.

Joline's bulky frame bumped Cybil slightly as she placed her hand on Cybil's shoulder. Her voice was soft and maternal. "My poor girl, there is not much you can do. There are other men that need attending to." Cybil did not stir. "Cybil, did you hear me?"

Cybil looked up. "Yes."

"Good. Off with you. You have rounds to do. I'll keep an eye on him. Although I can't imagine he's going anywhere."

Cybil gave Myles's forehead another dab then departed.

Joline looked at Myles then moved her mouth to his ear. "I can let you in on a secret. Since you can't hear me. She's taken to you. She's like a Florence Nightingale spending every free minute caring for you. For the life of me, I can't tell why." She dipped the cloth and dabbed his forehead. She chuckled softly. "Maybe it's the twinkle in your eye or you have better flour in you than the other doughboys."

Tony coughed. "You know I can hear you. What's wrong with my flour?"

Joline laughed.

CHAPTER 20

RECOVERY

Myles lay in the dark, his youthful face illuminated only by the soft light of a lantern. The lantern's flame danced inside without anyone to see. When he opened his eyes he found Cybil slumped over, fast asleep with a book on her lap. The Kerosene lantern rested on the floor next to her foot. She looked ragged as if she hadn't slept in days. Tony was missing from his cart beside him. *How long have I been out? I remember seeing goofy images floating around of that baby-faced, bald, bucktooth yellow kid. Wonder what the kid would say if anything about the war if he was still drawn today. Well, Hully gee here's to you, Say? Dis war is great stuff? I don't tink so.* He shook his head. *Focus.*

An itch in the back of his throat. He noticed a white porcelain pitcher of water with perspiration dripping from it on a tray table across the room. He looked at Cybil. *Poor thing. I can't wake her. She looks like she can use the rest. Maybe I can get out of bed and fetch it myself. Hop for it on my good foot? Nah, I'd slip and bust my lip open. That'll wake her up for sure.* Myles fought the craving to go for the pitcher and guzzle its contents. He stared at the ceiling. He wished the yellow kid to appear to entertain again if only to escape his boredom. The kid did not reappear but sleep caught him.

Myles woke with the morning light. Cybil was nowhere to be seen, nor was the pitcher. A middle-aged doctor wearing a tailored grey suit came to examine him. The doctor's brown hair speckled with gray was thinning severely revealing the start of a bald dome. He adjusted his spectacles.

"Marvelous. You looked like a goner a few days ago," The doctor said. "Your trench fever is broken and your foot does not seem to be infected. Thank God." The doctor drew a metal flask from his pocket and took a quick sip. Capped it then returned it to his pocket. "I am sending you back to the rear to recover in a real hospital."

"What do you mean by a real hospital?" Myles asked.

The doctor moved closer to Myles. Myles caught the rank breath of alcohol as the doctor spoke, "One with walls instead of a tent flap. You deserve the right care, I don't want you to lose your foot than end up a cripple. I'll send you out today. Probably not an enjoyable ride but the transport will get you there in one piece. They can do more for you than we can do here. They'll fix you up real good." The doctor's voice softened. "Also, it will take time to heal and we will need your bed for future arrivals."

Cybil entered. The doctor turned to her. "Nurse, this soldier needs to be cleaned up. I am putting orders in today for him to get out of here. Not sure when his ride will be here, but I don't want him coming out of here stinking like a fish." He turned to Myles. "No offense to you, boy."

Myles inhaled deeply through his nose. The doctor's observation was correct.

"Yes, sir," Cybil said. She approached Myles.

The doctor moved in front of her. "Not you. They need extra staff at site B. Pass these instructions along before you go."

Cybil's jaw set. She pressed her lips together as she looked at Myles. In a flicker, her eyes looked like they would well up.

"Cybil," Myles whispered to her. Cybil turned and without looking back departed.

"Don't worry." The doctor winked. "Plenty of pretty nurses to see when you get there." He took another nip from his flask then left.

Myles was transported via ambulance to the Town of Chantilly in the Somme area of Northern France. The town derived its name from Cantillius, a Roman who built the first villa there. The town managed to stay out of the war with the exception of Sept 3, 1914, when the German army invaded but caused no real destruction.

His destination was the hotel Spoelberch de Lovenjoul. The building was built before the French Revolution and spent most of its life as a boarding school for girls. Recently the hotel was a record library until August 1914. To aid in the war effort, museum collections were evacuated with those of the neighboring Condé museum and it was converted to a hospital.

On arrival, Myles's foot was painfully examined then X-rays were taken of it. The X- rays revealed no bone loss, but several fractures. His soft tissue damage and fractures would heal dependent on his body's ability to mend.

A wheelchair ride brought him to his recovery room. The small room was shared with four patients. Each patient had a wood-framed bed with a mattress and clean linen. These beds were a slice of heaven compared to accommodations in the trenches.

After a few days of bed rest, his pain subsided considerably, and most importantly his foot did not become infected. His foot would be staying with him. Whether it would function correctly was yet to be determined. The big question was would he be able to return to service. If he could not, he would get a ticket home. His ability to bear weight on his foot would answer that question. He hoped that once he bore weight on his foot, then he could walk, after walking he would be able to return to his unit. He prayed his hope would turn into reality and that he would march again beside his friends. Hope is formidable, but in the end, it's a promise that may not be honored by reality.

Test day, whether he could bear any weight, came. Myles was pushed in a wooden wheelchair that looked like one used for dining but with large wheels attached. A nurse, while humming an unrecognizable song, pushed him. She was a thin woman with grey hair wearing a clean white uniform. She was American and as sweet as apple pie. He never asked her name but after a few visits, he affectionately called her "Mom." Mom took a liking to Myles also and took an interest in making his stay at the hospital more comfortable. She found out Myles liked chess. Although she trounced him even more than his father ever did, Myles picked up some valuable new skills he would use against his father when he returned.

Mom wheeled him into the hallway just outside the room used for physical therapy, nicknamed the torture room. She took on a motherly expression. "Now I sent a colleague to fetch a cane for you to use. She should be returning soon. This will be your first attempt to walk. Take it easy, mind you. Rome wasn't built in a day."

Myles smiled affectionately. "Yes, Mom,"

The colleague indeed returned. Myles's face dropped. It was Cybil holding a polished maple wooden cane. His face turned flabbergasted and red.

Cybil's auburn hair was pristine, her face stoic, her slim body poised but there was no hiding the grin in her eyes. "Oh my! Myles, is it? I'm chuffed to bits to see you."

"Not sure what chuffed to bits means, but I'm glad to see you too."

Mom looked at Cybil and Myles suspiciously. "I see you two know each other. You two can footle conversation later. We have work to do."

Myles cleared his throat, "Hey, Cybil, would you like to stick around and watch the show? I'm about to take my first steps."

"I wouldn't miss it," Cybil teased. "But let's go before she gets the blue devils."

Mom held the door open as Cybil pushed Myles into the room. The room revealed various therapy equipment and lifting weights that stood along the walls. The hardwood floors were heavily polished. Any more polish and one would see their reflection in them.

Mom handed Myles the cane. She then removed his socks. "A little chilly but this should help you grip the floor better. Be careful, they went a little nuts with the floor polish." Mom continued with a hint of concern in her voice. "Now slowly raise and attempt to put weight on your foot."

Cybil stood ready to support his weight if necessary. Myles gripped the cane and used his good leg to rise, managing not to place any weight on his injured foot yet. He then stood up fully placing both feet on the floor. The wounded foot felt like it had a heartbeat of its own. He curled the toes of his injured foot. This caused shooting pain. He managed to turn his grimace into a marvelous fake smile, but his eyes fooled no one. *Ready or not.*

"Now when you're ready, try taking a step," Cybil spoke gently.

He took a step gripping his cane tightly. He felt a flash of pain like a dagger stuck into his foot. After 6 steps he could not bear the torment any longer. He froze, his face now succumbing to a grimace.

"Now that's enough for today." Mom said. "As I said before, Rome wasn't conquered in a day. You can wheel yourself around now. Every few hours I want you to take one step." She locked eyes and spoke firmly. "One step."

"The hallways of the hospital will be your daily marathon, Pheidippides," Cybil said.

"A Pheidippides I am not," Myles harrumphed, "but I will do my best. I think." He paused. "I think of myself more as a gladiator."

Cybil smiled. "Your Knackered, now let's get you off to rest.

"Cybil, bring him back to his room," Mom said.

Myles sat down in his wheelchair. He felt elation as the pressure released from his foot.

A knock at the door.

A doctor wearing back suit pants, a white shirt, a bow tie, and an oversized white coat entered. He spoke with a heavy Scottish accent. "Take me back to blighty, ah see written on ye face. Ye'v taken a few steps th'day. Good fur ye." The doctor gave a fatherly look. "Ah wanted ye to know ah wull be giein' ye an evaluation in three weeks to evaluate yer progress. Ye will either be fit tae return tae yer unit or be sent home. Yerr's foot wis badly wounded. Ye hae bin stitched up 'n' infection haes nae spread, but ah just don't know if oor efforts hae bin enough tae git ye back fightin' th' Hun. Yer have been wounded in the service of ye country. Yer land owes ye a stoatin deal o' gratitude. If ye can not return ye deserve tae haud yourself up with pride." He patted Myles's shoulder firmly then departed.

Myles sighed, his head fell into his hands. *Three weeks?* After six painful steps, he couldn't imagine enough recovery that would return him back to the line.

Cybil caught Myles's look of defeat. She bit her lip in thought. Gently, she touched his neck with her hand. The feeling sent a shiver down his spine. "To help give you extra motivation, a horse race nearby will take place in less than three weeks. It will be a jolly good time. I would like you to escort me if it suits you, but you must be able to walk to accept my invitation."

Mom gave Cybil the tiniest wink. "This race sounds like fun. Locals have told me Chantilly horse racing is some of the best in the world. You don't want to miss it."

Mom caught the fire in Myles's eyes when he first saw Cybil. She wondered what was more motivating, the race or escorting Cybil. She knew Myles and was aware he had a sweetheart but she also was a believer in "all is fair in love and war."

The hope of a quick recovery beaded Myles's skin like dew on a morning stone. He felt it radiate through his blood. Hope he could grab onto besides his cane.

Myles put on his best smile. "I would love to escort you. It'd be nice to have a change of scenery. I've been bored out of my skull here."

Mom feigned a look of offense. "Bored out of your skull?

Myles laughed. "It's boring to lose all the time to you in chess, but I do appreciate the company."

"You better do a better job than your chess play."

Myles gripped his cane tightly then pointed it in the air. "I promise to work my tail off."

"That's the spirit. Soldier, you have your mission. Now let's wheel you back to your room for some rest."

Over the next few days, Myles took more and more steps. Maybe a few more than he should have. He fought through the pain. The sweat from his efforts veiled any tears he shed. He thought he would need an iron will, but it appeared iron wasn't strong enough. He decided to become steel.

Cybil continued to encourage his efforts telling him how much excitement it would be at the race and that he wouldn't be going unless he could escort her. The doctor with the thick Scottish accent caught wind of Myles's hard work and set his evaluation that decided Myle's fate till the day after the race. Through encouragement and steely effort, he became physically and mentally stronger. Although with a modest limp, the day before the race with the aid of a cane he was able to move at a normal walking pace. He passed the test to take Cybil to the race; he would know soon if he passed the test to return to warfare.

CHAPTER 21

THE RACE

Under a cloudless sky, sunlight poured forth over the Chantilly Racetrack bathing the lush green grass of the flat track. The beautiful beige-colored Chantilly castle loomed in the background of the track. It was a beautiful day for a race. The heat of the day had just passed its peak, and a gentle breeze helped push away the humidity. Surrounding the track was a crowd of onlookers, mostly women in a 3:1 ratio. Although there was no official dress code nearly all the women wore sundresses in their favorite pastels with decorative, extravagant hats. The men dressed in their Sunday best suits. Observing the spectacle, you could not imagine there was a war going on that gripped all of Europe.

Horse racing had been canceled due to war and nearly half the jockeys and trainers were gone. The *Sociede d' Encouragement*, the governing body of French racing, persuaded the military to begin allowing some meetings to take place. Recently these locations were extended to include Chantilly. There were many racetracks in France, but Chantilly was one of the oldest and most loved.

The race crowd filled the stands with chatter, making it nearly impossible to hear any conversations. Myles sat on a folded wooden chair on a well-constructed grandstand. To his right side sat Cybil on a similar chair. He was dressed in a borrowed doctor's dark brown suit. The suit was a little loose on Myles because of his size. Cybil was dressed in a pink silk dress with an oversized hat with several black feathers in it. All beautiful women give an aura of sexual attraction. Yet she had a confidence about her that made what was inside desirable also. She was captivating. *I wonder what Kathy's up to right now. I wonder what she would think of Cybil. I can imagine she would be a tad jealous. Cybil's only a friend, isn't she?*

The race was about to begin. Nine horses stood in tight white painted wooden stalls with a gate that would swing open just after a shot was fired. Jockeys sat on their horses, eyes fixed forward in anticipation of the shot. They looked small and fragile compared to the large powerful horses they were about to ride. Regardless of their height, if you could see their faces, you would know they were highly trained professionals to be taken seriously.

A loud crack from a pistol rang out. The gate doors opened and the racers were off. The horses ran at full speed, muscles ripping from exertion. Three horses after the first lap broke from the pack ahead of the others. It was going to be a tight race. The jockeys worked to extend and constrict their legs with their body weight to create more speed. Their horses tore the ground kicking off clumps of earth and grass in their wake. As the lead pack was on the final lap, the horses all appeared to be neck and neck. Halfway to the finish, two horses broke off from the lead pack. Their jockeys lowered themselves as much as possible, struggling to gain any advantage they could. The crowd, their eyes glued to the race, cheered and roared as the two leaders raced toward the finish, then silence as the crowd held a collective breath. It was impossible to see a clear winner. In the remaining few seconds, the chestnut-colored stallion inched out slightly ahead of its competitor. The distance grew to several feet as it took the win. The momentary silence shattered as the crowd howled and applauded. During the jubilation, the winning jockey took his horse for a victory lap in a lazy trot around the track. You couldn't make out his face well but if you did you would have seen a face swelled with the ecstasy of the moment.

Myles and Cybil followed the crowd as it gathered around a wheeled podium, pulled out by horses at the edge of the track, to see the trophy ceremony. Because of Myles's slow gate, they were sandwiched in the middle of the crowd barely able to see the spectacle. The trophy was a beautiful silver cup sitting on a small wooden table. In the tight crowd, Myles's hand accidentally touched Cybil's and he jerked it away out of reflex. Cybil noticed his movement, grabbed his hand in hers then pushed closer to the platform with a few "excuse me"s. Myles allowed himself to be pulled.

The trophy was presented with a great show. The winning horse was handed to a stable hand then the jockey climbed the podium. A bottle of champagne was shaken then popped open by the winning horse's trainer to spray on the winning jockey. The remaining drink was subsequently poured into the trophy cup. The soaked jockey took several generous gulps then passed it up to his trainer. The trainer was a tall, stout man in striking contrast to the short, thin jockey. The display of happiness was the most entertainment Myles had seen in a while. A beacon of joy and laughter radiated from the spectators. He had forgotten there were moments like this. Fond memories from his childhood of winning sports games returned. He relished his escape in the moment.

The ceremony ended and the crowd dissipated. The winning jockey followed the direction of the crowd and his horse's reins were now passed to his trainer.

Cybil pointed at the horse. "Would you like to see the horse up close?" She whispered, "I know the trainer. His name is Harry." She spoke with great enthusiasm, her voice close to his ear.

Myles raised an eyebrow. "You know the trainer?"

"Sure, he worked with my family's horses a few years back. We had a stubborn mare named Poppy that gave him quite a jolly run for his money."

Myles and Cybil followed the winning horse as it was led to the stables. Myles, conscious of his limp, tried carefully to avoid it as much as possible.

A strong smell of horse manure greeted them as they entered the stall. The trainer was beginning to brush the horse. Harry reminded Myles of pictures he had seen in the newspaper of the British Prime Minister David Lloyd George. His white hair was combed well, his upper lip covered with a full mustache. The only noticeable difference was a long, pointed nose.

The trainer's eyes lit up when he noticed Cybil approaching. "My lady Cybil," he said with a thick British accent. "I didn't think to see you here today. Bloody nice to see you if you ask me."

Lady? Myles thought he heard the title incorrectly then it was repeated.

"My lady would like to meet Stepper. One of the finest stallions I've worked with." He patted and stroked the horse's neck. "Aren't ye, boy?" He glanced at Myles and gave a sniff from his nose. Myles thought he caught a disapproving look. "Who is your gentleman friend?"

"This is Myles, he was wounded at the front line. I thought it would be great fun to bring him to a race."

The trainer reached out and shook Myles's hand. It was a firm handshake, too firm; the strong grip of the shake lasted a few moments. Harry nodded to Myles. "I thank you for your service, your parents must be proud." Harry turned to Cybil. "Do bid your father a good greeting for me next time you see him."

"I'm afraid I won't be seeing him anytime soon, not until this horrid war is over at least. He didn't take a liking to me volunteering as a nurse."

Harry looked stunned.

"It wasn't right to sit and relax during the war while others go off and help," Cybil said.

"A nurse?" Harry exclaimed, "Well, good for you. I don't suppose your family was pleased to let you go. Losing such a valuable gem. Wherever did you receive your nurse training?"

"I trained in Manchester a little after the war began. The training wasn't easy. At first, I fainted at the sight of blood, but gradually I became proper." Cybil's face beamed with pride. "It was a struggle with my father, but here I am." She gently stroked the horse on the head. The horse neighed and tapped his feet.

"Cybil is a great nurse," Myles blurted out. The passion in his eyes attested to it.

"Yes, I'm sure she is." Harry did not turn to face Myles. He simply stared at the horse with a blank expression. His voice diminished as if he were talking to himself. "This war is a nasty business. I long for Chantilly to go back to the way it was before this war. Alas, it will never be the same. Many joined the 18th British Battalion, for soldiers with height less than regulations. Trainer George Batchelor, who has four daughters, lost his son in the Somme and Herbert Attwood the boy on his stable staff." He sighed, wiped his brow. "I must take my leave. Need to cool him down and give him a bath. Good day to you, Lady Cybil." He sniffed. "And a good day to you, Myles."

As soon as Harry was out of view, Myles eyed Cybil. "A lady? Not that it matters but maybe you could have mentioned this to me."

Cybil harrumphed. "Lady, it's a meaningless title. What does it mean to be a lady anyway? I enjoy my occupation as a nurse and being a lady is not what I chose to think about." He felt her gentle hands touch his arm. He shivered. "Myles, I have grown rather fond of you. I value our friendship. It's clear this world is going through a new age, but would you have treated me differently knowing that I was a lady?"

Myles rolled his eyes. "I will be honest with you. Maybe it's my American side talking, but truthfully I could care less." His voice softened. "I am fond of you as well. He touched her hands gently with his fingertips. I don't know what it is about you but I'm captured."

Cybil looked exuberant. "Well, flattery will get you nowhere, but actions will. Would you mind escorting me back to the hospital? I'm feeling rather knackered. I'll pay for a cab to fetch us back."

A few cabs were lingering by the track to give rides. Myles found a motor carriage, spoke to the driver and they were off. It was an uneventful ride.

Just as the hospital approached, Cybil leaned close to his ear. "I must admit, secretly I want you to fail your physical exam tomorrow so you do not go back to the fighting. I don't understand. So much effort to recover only to go back and risk your life again."

"Hhmmm, don't reckon I really know how to respond. I'm committed to serving as you are in the war effort. Although I admit my life will be in considerably more danger than yours." He flashed a warm smile. "I'll kick the Kaiser butt and ain't gonna let anything happen to me."

"Well, you better be safe." Her face turned serious.

The look on her face flashed Myes memories of Kathy's face as she sunk her nails into him with the words "You better return to me." He also remembered the promise that he would return home safely. *Return to her.*

"I give you permission to write to me if you are inclined to do so," Cybil said

"I surely will write as often as I can," Myles promised. *Would be nice to receive more letters.*

The cab arrived at the converted hospital, *Spoelberch de Lovenjoul.* The building was doing its service for the war effort. Millions of people across Europe were doing their part. Myles would have his answer the next day, what part he would play. Would it be back to the front with his unit or to be sent back home? It was in God's hands now.

CHAPTER 22

STAY OR GO

Although notably worn, the chair Myles sat on still held its character of being made by hand. Elegant, ornate details were carved into the polished back of the chair. He studied the floral pattern to help his breathing and focus on anything but the small waiting room he sat in. There wasn't so much claustrophobia but the anticipation of entering the dark stained wooden door at the end of the room. Beyond that door was the doctor's office where his fate would be sealed. His mind searched for a peaceful place but it found none. The grandfather clock on the floor chimed that it was 9 AM. He swallowed, stared at the clock, *tick-tock-tick-tock*. Any moment the veil of anxiety would be torn open when he was called inside that door.

Myles felt the itch of his olive drab wool uniform, he knew what returning to war meant, and the hellfire he would be facing, but he puzzled over what he would do if he was determined unfit for duty. *I can propose to Kathy? I'm still committed to her, ain't I. Find a job? I'm not working at my father's mill, maybe another? Work my way up.* His thoughts drifted to Cybil. *What chance is there?* He admitted to his heart he was in love with her, but what future could a poor American boy give to a lady from Britain. He could not begin to fathom the relationship working out.

He gently squeezed the arms of the chair. An urge to get up and pace called to him but he did not want to move his injured foot any more than necessary before his examination.

The doctor's door slowly creaked open. Biting his lip, Myles tried to relax.

A thin nurse dressed in white motioned him inside. "The doctor will see you now."

With a deep breath, he stood up and followed her through the doorway into the doctor's office doing his best not to show a limp. The doctor he recognized, the one with the thick Scottish accent. He stood wearing a white coat over his British military uniform.

The doctor glanced at the nurse. "Mary, please shut th' door behind ye." The nurse exited the room. The doctor motioned to a chair. "Please hae a seat. Tis Myles, is it nae?"

Myles sat down on the chair. "Yes, sir it's Myles. I never caught your name."

"Captain Wilson o' his majesty's airmie at yer service, ye can call me Hugh. Ye know ye kin let go o' yer breath 'n' breath."

"I'll breathe when the examination is over with."

"Myles, let me hae look at yer foot." He lifted Myles's pant leg and pulled off Myles's sock. "Well, na sign oo' infection. It didn't think thare wid be any. I've seen ye walk in and well you may have a limp fur a while tae be sure, but ah see na reason nae tae sign off that ye'r fit for duty. Ye will in time hae a full recovery although ye will carry thae scars fur life. Ye kin return tae th' line." His voice noticeably weakened. "Ye have performed yer duty to yer country. I know whit tis lik' over there." He grabbed his clipboard. "Ye'r in a combat unit. Dae yer feelin' ye'r ready tae return tae th' front again?" He looked deep into Myles's eyes. "If yer feelin' yer nae physically or mentally ready ah will marc ye unfit 'n' ye kin return home"

Myles's eyes bulged. *What is he saying? Is he offering me a way out? What should I do?* Myles quieted his mind then listened to his heart. "I want to return to the front. My brothers are there. As long as I can fire a shot, I want the opportunity to fight with them."

Hugh closed his eyes and let out a long breath then gave a half-hearted smile. "A transport bus wull be arriving tae tak' recoveries back tae their units this afternoon. Ah wull reserve yer name."

Myles shuttered, felt like his heart skipped a beat. "So soon?"

"Ah know it's short notice bit th' transport only swings by once a week. Ah wull give ye some medication tae ease any continued pain." He reached down and wrote a note on a piece of paper from his desk and handed it to Myles. "Give this to the nurse on yer wey out, tis for opium. She wull fetch it fur ye. Unfortunately, I'm at liberty only tae give ye a month's supply. Shortages. Ah wull give orders tae restrict ye tae light duty fur six weeks. Although mah instruction wull likelie be ignored."

"Thank you, sir." Myles stood up straight then snapped a salute. The salute was returned. Myles turned and left the room. He handed the handwritten note to the nurse and she returned with a small glass bottle with tiny dark brown pills in it. Myles placed the bottle in his pocket then sauntered off to his room.

He did not get too far. The entrance to his room was blocked by Cybil. She stared at Myles, her eyes open wide, full of emotion and an uneasy smile on her face. "What is the answer? Is it war or is it home?"

"To war," Myles murmured.

Cybil did her best to hold her smile but it collapsed. She looked down. "I will miss our intrigues together."

Myles's voice cracked, "So will I, I promise to write to you. I'll fill you in on all my adventures."

She looked up then kissed him on the cheek, her eyes said she wanted so much more. This kiss sent warmth to Myles's heart that tugged the strings.

"I leave first thing in the morning. A transport bus will be fetching me." Myles said.

"That soon?" Cybil gasped softly.

"I'm sorry."

Cybil's deep blue eyes bore into Myles's eyes. "If I may be so bold. Your friendship has been most kind. I have it in my mind that our paths may not meet again, but if destiny brings us to each other again I would very much like to see where the path takes us."

"Cybil, I am grateful for our friendship. You helped me recover more than just my foot, you helped lift up my heart and spirits when I could easily have slipped into despair. I don't know if our paths will cross again. Maybe it was fate that we met, let's leave it up to it and see if we are destined to meet again."

An awkward silence followed. They both looked into each other's eyes then mutually embraced. A hug of strong arms that for a brief moment held back any of their worries. Cybil pushed herself out gently. "Well, I guess it's goodbye. Take care of yourself." Cybil sniffled, stood straight then walked away. She held back tears until she turned the corner, then they became a waterfall.

Myles entered the recovery room he called home for the past few weeks to sort out his few personal items. He bagged what little he brought, an extra uniform and toiletry items. He tightened the drawstring on his denim blue barracks bag then stretched out on his bed. His mind pondered what his unit would be doing right now. *Probably crawling through the mud. If they knew I had a ticket home, how many would think I was nuts for coming back?*

"Leaving?" A sleepy, deep voice said from a patient on the bed directly across from Myles. Myles recognized Frank's distinctive voice. It was the kind of deep voice that belonged to an opera. Myles had shared more than a few laughs with him.

Myles stood up and looked at Frank's heavily bandaged face with one eye showing.

"News travels fast," Myles said.

"Oh, nobody's told me. I may only have one eye, but it sees pretty good. You'll be back to the fighting. Gosh, I wish I was going with you. With one eye gone and a crippled hand, I don't think they'll even consider me for a desk job. Not that I haven't asked. The docs only give me smiles when I ask them. I'll likely get a ticket home sooner for my efforts."

Myles walked over to Frank's bed and took a seat at the edge. "Frank, you served your country." He lowered his voice. He turned his head to stare at a patient sleeping across from Frank, missing part of one leg up to his knee. "And you'll be returning walking on your own two feet."

"I guess you're right," Frank said.

"Besides," Myles said, "The girls back home will all want to kiss a hero. They'll be lining up for yah."

"Yup, I'm sure that'll be the case. That's good. I ain't no Casanova. Although I sound like one, I have always been shy with the girls." He suppressed a laugh, then his voice turned serious. "Myles, you stay alert. Watch out for bullets, you hear me?"

Myles reached out then patted Frank's shoulder.

"You got it, bud."

Myles returned to his bed. He pulled out his Bible he kept under his pillow. He removed his bookmark and read from Exodus. The Book of Exodus teaches about God's deliverance of the Israelites from slavery in Egypt and the requirements of the law given to them in the Ten Commandments at Mt. Sinai.

After reading, he took out his cherished photos from home. As he flipped through the photos his heart pained to see his family again. The pain was a weight to his heart that would not be lifted until he saw them again. *I chose to stay.*

That night sleep came late. It took time for his body to defeat the thoughts racing in his mind. When his eyelids closed, he thought he felt a presence near him. As if he was being watched. Words burned in his head as if he were only a listening device. *There are ten commandments given to men, but all of these are summed up in the two greatest commandments of all, Love the Lord your God with all your heart, with all your soul, with all your mind... and love your neighbor as yourself. Here is an example. To willingly risk one's life for another does follow... to love your neighbor. The sons of men often ask is it ok to kill in war and still love your neighbor? The answer: as long as it is necessity, not desire, which slays the enemy.*

CHAPTER 23

RETURN TO THE FRYING PAN

Myles plopped himself down with his barracks bag on a hard wooden bench outside the front entrance to the hotel *Spoelberch de Lovenjoul* then waited for the transport bus that would take him back to his unit. He was wearing his helmet and freshly cleaned uniform. He patted his bag then double-checked the button on his front pockets. His Bible and photos were secure in one; his bottle of pills was secure in the other. He was ready for pick up.

He glanced at the front entrance to the hotel, a few feet away. It was not so bustling this early in the morning. He was the only soul outside the entrance. A strong breeze blew, knocking a cluster of colorful leaves off a nearby tree. He watched the leaves as they fluttered to the earth. They hit the ground softly making no sound.

He leaned back on the bench and wiggled his body to get more comfortable. He wiggled his toes in his boot and felt a dull ache. *Still there, I hope you're ready for work again.* He began to tap his feet lightly to "It's a Long, Long Way to Tipperary." It was a popular song that had nothing to do with war but was actually a humorous account of a lonely Irishman lost in London, but somehow it fit his melancholy mood.

A battle bus painted a utilitarian green with a decent amount of rust rumbled up the long driveway to the entrance. The bus windows had been replaced with olive drab-painted wood boards. A few flecks of bright red paint could be seen if you looked close enough. He wondered where the bus made its stops before the war. *Probably in London.* The bus stopped.

The driver, a mostly toothless man with an unlit pipe in his mouth, opened the door. Myles handed the driver a slip authorizing his trip and confirming his destination then looked for a seat in the packed vehicle. He found one open seat next to a dark-haired American soldier with pearly white teeth. He looked like a movie star but smelled like he hadn't bathed in weeks. Myles wished he could open the windows for fresh air. Especially when the driver lit his pipe.

It was a long ride with the bus bouncing up and down. It took several hours with multiple fuel stops until the bus made its way towards the front lines. A few miles from the fighting the bus began to make stops to drop off its passengers. Myles was one of the three passengers remaining when the bus reached his stop. The door screeched open.

"Private Myles," called the bus driver. "Your stop." Myles grabbed his bag then departed the bus. He stepped on the concrete sidewalk into the center of a bustling French town. The driver pulled out his pipe and gave a toothless smile. "Stay here, someone from your unit will come by to collect you. They should have been telephoned."

"How long?"

"Just wait. They'll come," the driver replied, placing his pipe back in his mouth, a thin wisp of smoke curling out of its bowl. He slammed the door shut.

Myles watched the bus knock and jerk away then observed his surroundings. The town, most likely sleepy and quiet before the war, was now expanded way beyond its capacity. The clamor of noise and smells of the town filled the crowded streets. Civilians and soldiers bustled everywhere with purpose. His gut tempted him to explore but he refrained, fearing his unit would come to retrieve him, find he wasn't there, and leave.

He stood waiting on the sidewalk. His stomach growled and he was thirsty. It was late afternoon. He hadn't had anything since his breakfast of tea and biscuits with jam and hadn't thought to bring any food. While in recovery he was spoiled with 3 full meals a day and occasional snacks. His new food accommodations would not be so nice but his body didn't know this.

A cheery voice called out, "Myles, that you?" Myles turned. He recognized Steven from his platoon with two rifles slung over his back. Steven radiated energy the way a squirrel constantly appears in movement.

Myles grinned. "You bet. What did you do? Forget about me, I've been waiting here forever."

"It took longer than I thought to get here. That's all. Gee, looks like you gained a few pounds on your vacation. How was your stay at the Biltmore?"

"Well..," Myles attempted to get a word out.

"We've been giving old Fritz a run for their money. A few didn't make it. Matt and Jamison." He shook his head. "We've got a new promotion to platoon Sergeant. You'll know him. Well, it's a long walk to our position. I hope you can manage. I heard you were shot badly in the foot?" Steven winked.

Myles couldn't help but frown.

"Don't be sore with me," Steven said. "They are where they are. Whatcha think we would drive you back to the front line in a bus? Strap your bag to your back. Oh, and here." He handed one of the rifles over to Myles. Myles automatically checked the serial number. It was not his rifle, but it appeared in good shape.

"You have any food with you?" Myles said.

"Don't know if you like it, but I've been saving this." He pulled out a wrapped bar. "Got some chocolate leftover from my ration."

"Chocolate! Are you friggin' kidding me? Give it over."

Myles undid the wrapper and ate the bar greedily. It kind of tasted like chocolate but not the taste he was used to. Very grainy and bitter, but a feast to a hungry stomach.

"Give me your canteen," Myles said pleasantly.

Steve handed it over.

Myles removed one of his little brown pills and swallowed it with the water.

"Lead the way," Myles said.

They walked out of the busy town and went straight into the woods. The woods became thick as they moved further. The rich smell of the forest floor held a strong odor of life and sap. Myles walked carefully to avoid exposed roots or branches. He knew a bad slip would ruin his recovery. They walked up and down hills at a steady pace. Myles's foot began to ache and a phantom tearing sensation threatened to overwhelm him. Steven noticed the pained facial expressions from Myles and called for a halt after a particularly savage grimace.

Myles slipped off his boot. No blood soaked through the thin wrappings. He took another pill to suppress the pain. A squirrel passed by him and ran up a large oak tree, carrying an acorn in his mouth. *Squirrelling nuts away for the winter. Hell. Wish I could squirrel my pain away. A German could be sneaking up right behind me and I wouldn't even notice.* He put his boot back on then they continued. Steven set a new pace similar to that of a turtle's movement.

"It won't be long, Myles. Try and get your mind off the pain. Hey, did you meet any pretty nurses at the hospital?"

Myles couldn't help but smile. "Sure did, turns out she was a lady. Not a lady but a *lady*. Like you read in books. Why she took to me I'll never know. Maybe I was just so pathetic with my injury, maybe I was just so devilishly handsome."

"Probably the pathetic part," murmured Steven.

Myles snorted, "Ha, very funny."

The forest abruptly gave way to a large opening of tall grass that seemed to extend for miles. Tress to the left and right. Myles let out his fingers to caress the tips of the blades of grass. He casually looked up at the sky. The sun was just beginning to go down but the blue sky was still radiant and cloudless. He heard a humming sound overhead as if a bee's nest had been kicked. A squadron of airplanes flew overhead with red, white, and blue on the tails of the plane.

"What a sight," Myles said.

"French-made spads. Death from above. We've been seeing them more. Gonna help us wangle Fritz."

They watched the planes disappear.

Steven drummed his fingers on his helmet. "Would you ever fly in one? They sure give me the willies."

"Well, I th—."

"It's not too far now," Steven said. "And do keep a sharp eye, don't want the boys to mistake you for a Fritz."

Myles did his best to observe his surroundings but now constant foot pain made it difficult to focus. He plodded on seeing nothing.

After a modest distance, they heard the bolt of a rifle pulled back.

"Freeze! Don't take another step!" barked a deep voice.

Both men stopped. Myles instinctively pointed his rifle in the direction of the voice, his finger tightened against the trigger, but he did not squeeze. Steven kept his rifle lowered.

"Johnny!" bellowed a different voice.

"Appleseed," Steven said quickly.

The deep voice rumbled, "You fools get over here, gonna get yourself killed. We don't know where the Germans are hiding. We heard you guys coming a mile away."

Myles and Steven moved slowly toward the voice.

"Where the hell are they," Steven whispered.

The deep voice softened, "Keep quiet, we've advanced past two layers of the enemy's defenses but the third wall is out there. Don't want to whack the nest too early."

They continued towards the voice. They still did not see the man behind the voice—till they almost stepped on the man who was laying on his belly alongside a half dozen men. Myles immediately recognized him as Edward Boulanger, who the men called "Ed." He was well known for the large scar on his right cheek, not from combat overseas but from a broken bottle in a bar fight in Boston, MA.

"Ed, sorry, almost plum stepped on you!" Steven said. "You kno-"

"Hey dummies," Ed said. "You almost friggin' stepped on me. Keep your voices down and don't make any noise, you don't want to give our position away." Ed slowly got up then faced Myles. "Your back, aye. I've taken over Lance's platoon. I miss that SOB. How's your foot?"

"I can manage, Sarge. Here." He reached into his coat pocket, grabbed the doctor's note then handed it to Ed.

Ed sighed after reading the note, "Well, there's no light duty in a war zone, I can get you out of patrols but that's it. We need every man we can get. When the word is given, we're gonna move like bloody hell. Get ready to work. Oh, you will need this." Ed handed Myles a small shovel. "We're digging one-man defensive positions just deep enough to lay down and lookout." He pointed. "You'll dig your fox hole over there."

Myles looked at the shovel. Just the thought of using it made his foot ache. He felt the call for another pill pleading for him like a prince repeatedly calling for his Rapunzel to let down her golden hair. He resisted the temptation. He knew he had a limited supply of the miracle pill. Myles looked at his shovel then looked at the grassy spot he needed to dig out. *Dang.* He dropped his barracks bag to the ground and got to work. With his good foot, he stepped on the shovel digging into the earth. He bent over, moved the dirt then began to dig again.

With the sun waning the air grew chilly. He didn't notice until his work was done. He fetched an extra blanket from Ed then sat, exhausted in his dugout, wrapped in it.

His pals took turns visiting his position, sharing more than a few jokes and laughs at his expense. They enjoyed the story of his recovery, the horse race, and especially his new friend Cybil. He didn't tell them he could have received a ticket home. The men were not the same as he remembered. There was a sense of gloom about the men, subtle yet real. The war was at a turning point and the storm was coming. They wanted to survive it.

CHAPTER 24

THE PATH

November 9th, 1918. The American Yankee Division was advancing daily, clearing village after village in the Argonne region of France. Their battalions, although reduced in numbers and effective strength, were pushing forward slowly but surely in the face of heavy opposition. They were paused at present, digging in to prepare for a counteroffensive by the Germans.

The sun was just rising toward an empty sky. Myles was filthily mud-encrusted with a thick layer of dust covering his uniform. He had just finished digging out a hasty fighting position with his small trench shovel. He attempted to scrub some of the dirt out from his hair with his hands. He felt tiny rocks escape his scalp as he scrubbed. He was tired and despondent, like many wanting a respite from the squalor of war.

Myles reached for his coat laying on the leaf-covered ground. Most of the leaves had fallen off the trees now, giving a colorful blanket to the ground. He put on his coat and unconsciously curled his toes to test his injured foot. Only discomfort if he curled them too tightly. Night and day better. It was a blessing not to feel unsparing pain anymore, especially since he was out of pills for the pain. Myles stood up, unscrewed the cap from his canteen and took a large gulp of water then tipped it upside down. Finished. They had plenty of water, warm but still refreshing. However, the food was not plentiful. His stomach growled. His platoon was fed three times a day but the amounts in the food rations were not enough to match the men's physical exertion. Like Caesar's troops that crossed the Rubicon so long ago, the Yankee Division was not stopping.

It was obvious to the men that the war would end soon. It was clear to both armies, but they continued to slug it out like two brothers over an argument that neither would let go. Both armies fought to gain as much territory as they could, even after a specific cease-fire time and date was reached, precisely 11 a.m. on November 11, 1918. Although this was the chief reason both armies fought, maybe vengeance and the need to kill one last time played a role. Whatever the reason, bloodshed would continue to the last moment. The allies were instructed by their command to continue their advance till the final hour. Far away American commanders pushed for the advance, keeping their own hands clean. The advance did not stop the Germans from fighting back tooth and nail. They resisted with murderous machine guns and artillery fire, forcing the Americans to measure gains in yards. They threw everything they had remaining against the doughboys. Including reserve forces not previously committed before.

Sgt Edward Boulanger walked toward Myles. With his blackened face and dusty uniform, he looked like a coal miner just out of his hole. He puffed a fat cigar then made a poor attempt to blow out a smoke ring. He raised an eyebrow. "You want a cigar. I could spare one at least, saving a few for when they call the truce. I mean to celebrate."

Myles shook his head no. Ed continued, "Looks like I'm playing postman today. Two letters for you. You must be very popular back home. Can't remember the last time I got a letter. Well, I suppose it's because I stopped writing to anyone. If you ain't got anything nice to say, don't say it at all, I reckon. Maybe that had something to do with that."

"Gee, you think, sergeant?" Myles murmured.

Ed dismissed the comment with a wave. He handed the letters to Myles then departed.

Myles scanned the addresses. *Maybe a letter from Kathy finally.* The letters were from Lillian and Cybil. Myles tore open the envelopes.

> *Dear brother,*
>
> *I hope you are safe. I can't wait till you come home. I have no one to tease anymore. I wanted to tell you something. I was out with my friends in the park playing with my friends when I saw Kathy smooching with someone. I ran over to see who it was and Kathy told me to be quiet that she would tell you as soon as you returned. She didn't want to affect your mood while you're over there fighting in harm's way. I spoke to mom and dad and they left it up to me. Grandpa told me to remind you that there are plenty of fish in the sea. Anyway, I thought it wasn't right. I had to say something. I also know you would never forgive me if I kept the secret. The boy she locked lips with was your so-called buddy George. Anyway, you know now. Gotta run, gonna take Shilo for a walk.*
>
> *Love,*
> *Lilly*

Myles staggered backward a step, his mind swirling with shock, his hands tightened into fists as any dreams about Kathy melted away. *Drat, this explains why she hasn't been writing to me. How could she do this to me? I was going to ask her to marry me when I got home.* He took a deep breath then opened the letter from Cybil.

Dear Myles,

I miss you. Your presence brought joy to my heart that is hard to describe. I have a confession. You may have figured it out. After I met you I transferred to the Hotel Spoelberch de Lovenjoul. I told them I needed a break from being so close to the action. I admit I did pull a few strings. It helps to be a lady. I notice every time you hear this title of 'lady' you get squeamish. I am a woman first. I don't care what my family says. The world is changing. This great war changes everything.

I did not have the courage to tell you in person my feelings towards you, but I appear to have more courage now away with a pen in hand. My heart is resolved. I love you. I know you have a girlfriend but I would like you to consider my affections. When the fighting ends I will go to my family's retreat in Newport, Rhode Island. Whether lovers or friends, I look forward to seeing you again.

Love,
Cybil

Myles sat down using his helmet as a seat. He placed both letters on his lap then massaged his temples. Whatever was there, real or something he imagined, was over with Kathy. *Funny, I didn't see a path before with Cybil. Now one is there. The path may not be clear and it may be a struggle to walk it, but does it matter as long as I reach the destination? First, though I have to make it to the starting point.*

A crack of rifle fire sounded. A tiny puff of dirt flew next to him. Myles threw himself into his freshly dug position. The letters flew through the air then scattered to the ground.

He could hear Ed close by yelling, "Get the F%$# down! Sniper!" Time seemed to stand still as Ed crawled to Myles with Corporal Eric Wilkenson, a hard-faced soldier nearby. "You see where the shot came from?" Ed said.

Myles shook his head. "I didn't get a good look at it, Sarge. I was getting my ass down."

Ed scowled. "We need another shot to pinpoint the bastard's position."

"Maybe somewhere over there in the tree line is my guess," Eric said. "He wouldn't be behind us."

"I have a plan," Ed said. "Eric and I will flush him out." He pointed to Myles. "And when he gets to you, take him down."

"You got it, Sarge!" Myles proclaimed.

Ed and Eric disappeared into the multi-colored foliage. Myles's heart raced as he scanned the foliage in front of himself. He wished he dug his hole a little deeper to hide from the sniper. He listened intently. He heard a crunching of leaves moving in his direction. He aimed with his rifle sight. A soldier in a grey uniform moved stealthily from tree to tree. He wore all sorts of leaves and branches attached to his uniform and helmet but his camouflage did not hide him from Myles. Myles took aim. A shot rang out. The shot missed. The German froze. Another shot. A spray of red. The German staggered and fell.

Myles approached the corpse. He stiffened under a wave of remorse. Poor soul to get it so close to the end of the war. He whispered a prayer, "Lord, watch over and guide this man's soul and please end this war before any more are lost on either side." Like a wisp of smoke, the sound of the words floated through the air. If a tree falls without anyone there to listen, was the sound made at all? Yes. Simply no one is there to hear it. All words that are spoken are known to heaven. And heaven delights to answer prayers if we ask not of our selfish desires.

CHAPTER 25

PRAYERS HEARD

In the sky above the war zone, a rumble of thunder was heard. The sound was odd coming from a cloudless sky, but not the strangest sound. Perhaps the most unique sounds were the sounds that were heard. The enemies were close to each other. Close enough to hear a loud sneeze. With a truce to start soon, there should have been bursts of laughter and sounds of celebration yet there was none. Sporadic rifle fire rang out back and forth with bangs and pops.

American intel continued to tell a German counter push was imminent. Despite the fruitlessness of an advance, the good sons of the German fatherland would follow orders to march possibly to their deaths until the war's bitter end. Every snapped twig or panic flight of an animal hidden in the undergrowth gave an eerie pause. A dark storm was brewing and would be released soon.

Myles lay prone in his shallow one-man fighting position observing the German lines surrounded by his brothers-in-arms to his left and right in similar positions. The Germans were well hidden in a woodline that extended past a large area of light vegetation. He was god-awful tired not to mention his uniform's pungent smell of sweat vinegar.

Ed crawled to Myles's position with an expression of fatherly concern on his face. "How is your ammo supply?"

"Sarge, I have six clips," Myles said.

Ed nodded. "Water?"

"At least half a canteen."

"Good. Don't rightly know if I could get you anything. But I'm keen on trying if you do need something. Ain't much here. I was able to find you an extra ink pellet for your trench pen." Ed handed a black pellet to Myles from his coat pocket.

Myles gave a warm smile. "Thanks, Sarg."

Ed returned the smile. "Pete had an extra one. He doesn't write as much as you." He cast his eyes towards the German positions. "This land district has been known before the time of Caesar. I wonder what stories this forest could tell about the changes through the years. I hear bears used to roam these woods about fourteen to fifteen years ago. Nothing but wildfowl now."

"Would love to catch a bird, and sink my teeth into one," Myles said. "The chow here is terrible at best."

"You'll have all the food you want soon," Ed said. "Mark me, they will fatten us up like piglets before they ship us back home. It will cover up the hunger we endured."

Home?" Myles said. "I know it hasn't been years, but I feel like I've been here for an eternity."

"Stay sharp, it will be over soon." Ed patted Myles's shoulder. "I feel you. Forever and a day."

Ed crawled off to check on more soldiers.

Myles lay on his back then scribbling a letter to Cybil.

> . . . and this is finally the tip of it. In 3 hours the war is going to be over. It appears unbelievable whilst I write this letter to you. I suppose we should be jubilant and excited. Instead, there is the darkness of a knife that grits our nerves, because

the bullets will not stop till the clock reaches 11 a.m. At this moment we sit in silence, in awe that the end is near. We slept underneath artillery fire and witnessed unspeakable carnage; we can hardly fathom nor comprehend the stillness. I long to see you in Newport.

Love,
Myles

Myles placed the letter into his pocket then he turned over on his belly. *Is this worth it?* He grabbed a handful of dirt as he peeked out in the direction of the Germans. He flicked the dirt away, then with both hands nestled his rifle against his shoulder. He looked at his rifle site. *Poor bastards, don't you know when you've been beaten. So brave and dutiful. Jerry's, you embrace death when you have the option to run from it. I understand the call, I chose to fight when I could have received a ticket home.* He shook his head. *To fight now! To kill now! The ticket of peace has been punched. It's murder on both sides.*

A sound bustled from behind Myles. He turned around quickly. A greyish brown deer, he noticed as a blur nearly smacked into him. It dodged at the last second before impact then bolted past him. It should have scared the living daylight out of him but instead, it made a grin spread to his lips. *Sure-footed even amidst the perils you face on earth.*

Franz was crouched in conversation with Hans and Lukas.

"And what of you?" Franz said to Hans.

Hans patted his belly. "After this is over I'm gonna have a big meal." He looked down at his stomach. "Don't reckon my family will recognize me."

"Besides that, you foot-slogger," Franz said. "Do you want to accomplish anything? Is there something now on your dream list?"

Hans let out a long breath. "Honestly, nothing. I just want to return to a simple life back home at the farm. I don't mind getting dirty. Dirt is easier to wash off than blood."

"I know what you mean," Franz said. "I can almost smell the peat now."

Both Franz and Hans looked at Lukas.

"Me, I look forward to teaching. I take my job seriously. The duty of a teacher is not to dump knowledge into my students but to plant seeds. Seeds that will grow into a blooming plant. There'll be a lot of fatherless children. I owe it to the fallen to do a good job."

"Look," Franz said. "Whatever the future brings it will be better than being here." He shook his head. "Let's focus on surviving so we can make it there. Keep yourselves and your men alive!"

Franz returned to his position. Franz rolled over on his back then finished a letter to his wife Erna and his two remaining daughters Herta and Anna.

> . . . . . . *I long to come home. I long to visit Emma at the cemetery. Although miles divide us, and we can not see each other, I feel you all in my heart. This war is over. Truly over, we have an exact time, yet we continue to press for gains. We have just been ordered to attack in a few minutes. Unspeakable! History might as well be a wave crashing on the shore, for men have learned nothing, but how to fill a grave. I fear this is not the war to end all wars, men will never learn. They will always march to the loss of their dreams. Many brave men here have lost their laughter and this I believe is the worst. I do not wish to trouble your hearts. If I do not cheat death, know that I will go to a place where joy and laughter never left.*
>
> *Love,*
> *Franz*

Franz folded the letter then placed it into his pocket. He aimed his rifle in the direction of the Americans. *Poor bastards, don't you know you have won. Doughboys, sent from a great distance to support your friends. Your storm won, why gamble now with your lives. Pull back. Does not the cool earth have enough gallant soldiers' blood?*

A beautiful red deer stag charged out of the thick brush in front of him. It slowed to a stop then raised its head to sniff the air. It was a truly majestic animal, proudly standing with the most beautiful horns. Its reddish-brown coat, darkening to grayish brown as winter approached, with lighter underparts and a light rump. It walked with an innocent grace showing no fear. Franz smiled. *Sure-footed even amidst the perils you face on earth.*

The deer produced a loud snort then bounded away.

CHAPTER 26

WHITE CAVALRY

One hour before the truce started, German artillery began to pound the Yankee Division with a bombardment that sounded like loud cracks of thunder. Traveling at the speed of sound the shells rained down without stopping as if every last one was being hurled. Hell was giving all it had left. Shell impacts hurled clumps of dirt from the ground and wood splinters from the trees. Under the barrage, the defenders curled up in their fox holes or found whatever cover they could find.

Myles lay in a fetal position, praying a shell did not find him. He watched as a shell landed nearby and sent earth with a man flying through the air. The mutilated corpse fell to the ground in a heap. Myles averted his eyes. *Doggone,* Myles thought, *to be killed less than an hour's breadth away from the end of the war. Lord, please continue to save me from the grim reaper cuz it ain't over yet.*

The bombardment was the least of his troubles, he knew the Germans would emerge from their holes and try to smash through the American line in an attempt to capture as much territory as they could grab before 11 a.m., the exact time the armistice went into effect.

The sounds of the barrage began to relent slowly then stopped with an eerie silence. Only clouds of smoke remained from the violent artillery strike and the smell of churned earth and burnt wood.

Behind the cover of the woods, the German First Army watched the bombardment. They had been reinforced with an entire division the night before. Traveling in the dark their movement was completely hidden. There was plenty of ammunition for the offensive. The fighting would end soon, so they could spend every last round. The Americans would be in for a surprise and would pay dearly. The Germans were packed in the brush like a can of sardines awaiting the signal to attack.

After the rumbling booms faded, Franz looked towards the American position. Plumes of black smoke billowed the air like a heavy fog. Only 60 yards away was the enemy. It would be a walk in the park against little resistance. He had no doubt the sheer number of soldiers with plenty of ammunition would wreak havoc against the Americans and make gains, but he was concerned for his men. He hadn't asked to become company commander, but that did not relieve him of responsibility. His men needed him. Their lives were in his hands. He was committed to everything in his power to keep them safe.

He lay on his belly, miserable, damp, and antsy to move. By his side lay his rifle, muzzle-up, showing a fixed bayonet. His arms tingled underneath his body and he rubbed them to bring back his circulation. He scanned the men of his company. Battle-hardened faces. The innocence of youth lost to war. The war would end soon. He would do his duty for his country but his mind was tormented with the why? Why was the war continuing? For a final few miles of territory. Maybe the Kaiser and the government care about needless scraps of land but not for these poor boys. In a cold sweat, heart racing, he waited for the order to charge.

"Aufladen!" Echoed loud. The Germans poured out of their positions like ants kicked from a nest. To his left and right, a tidal wave of grey uniforms covered the earth. Franz led in front of his company with orders not to pass him. A sound was made by hundreds of boots stomping the soft earth as the soldiers advanced. He waded his company out of the woods into an open field with little foliage. It looked like an abandoned farm field beginning to be reclaimed by nature. Across the field, the Americans started firing back. Franz motioned for his men to keep low.

Suddenly a strange barrage of sound erupted that oddly blared like many trumpets. Puzzlingly, the sound came not from their enemy but to their immediate right. The area was scouted before the bombardment and it should have been impossible for the enemy to hide there. Franz looked straight towards this trumpeting wondering what on earth was making this noise. His jaw dropped.

The sky opened up with a bright shining light; he followed the light down to see a cavalry column of several hundred British soldiers on the field. They wore shining white uniforms and each rode a brilliantly white horse. The cavalry rode slowly with dignity showing no shred of fear. At the front of the column was an officer with no helmet. This beautiful man held penetrating brilliant blue eyes. He looked like a statue chiseled out of marble. His blond hair sparkled giving an illusion of a halo around his head. Bullets whistled towards the cavalry. But no cavalry soldiers fell. The bullets either missed or had no impact.

Loud cracks from concentrated rifle shots opened up on the cavalry were deafening. Incredibly the cavalry in a lazy trot continued forward oblivious to any danger. *Sure-footed,* Franz thought as he watched the cavalry, *even amidst the peril surrounding them.*

Fear began to take hold of the Germans. The impossible was becoming real to them. It became apparent this was something unworldly. The column's leader kept his eyes forward, his face solid with confidence.

German eyes grew wide with terror; they began to slow down their fire. The attacking infantry closest to the column began to drop their rifles where they stood then fled back towards their lines. The entire German advance froze. Not all the Germans could see what was happening but they knew the battle plan had been dramatically altered. No battle ever went according to plan and this was an extreme example of that fact.

A large number of American soldiers also saw the spectacle of the white cavalry. In disbelief, they halted their fire afraid to hit the cavalry. Now they stood mouths gaping, pointing towards the column. They witnessed the Germans retreat from the cavalry by dozens, by hundreds, then by thousands.

Franz continued to stare dumbfounded as the German army disintegrated around him.

Hans grabbed him roughly by his arm and dragged him a few feet.

"Franz, Snap out of it," Hans said. "It's a retreat, let's go before the Americans open fire on us. Schnell!"

"W-What is happening," Franz stuttered.

Hans shook his head. "You've seen them. We're either dreaming the same dream or this is real. Either way, I don't think sticking around is a good idea."

Franz woke from the fog in his head to signal to his men to retreat. As he looked over his shoulder, he could still glimpse the white cavalry. The cavalry halted. The last memory was seeing the leader of the mounted men appear to look up slightly to the sky with a look of satisfaction on his face.

Jaw dropped in awe, Myles watched the white cavalry's leisurely ride. He stood up as did, with many others pointing at the column.

In a flash of light, the cavalry's white uniforms changed to white shining robes. The horses vanished. On foot, the former cavalry began to walk. Their feet are in simple tan leather sandals. They continued to walk until they reached the previous positions of the Germans. They froze. A loud crack of thunder followed by a long bolt of lightning ripped across the upper atmosphere. The sky began to darken as the sun was enveloped in dark clouds. In less than a blink, the cavalry vanished.

A powerful, and the most beautiful voice he had ever heard, spoke in his mind. *The intense prayers lifted to heaven from churches throughout the world have reached a crescendo. Heed these words. Nations for your own good, stop the means of acquiring more power, rather cooperate among the fraternity of mankind. Don't you know the decency of man and woman to love one another is the strongest power on earth? When you're all strong in love and maintain sure-footedness and devotion to God amidst the perils you face on earth, you will have an earth you're all happy with regardless of your origins, culture, or nation. May you go in peace today and remember to love one another as the Father loves you all.*

The dark clouds moved to reveal an ivory sun. It shone brilliantly. Those that looked up averted their eyes. The radiance of the light grew to a crescendo then flashed, shedding its whiteness to return to normal.

As soon as the cavalry departed there were many doubters. Did this really happen? Afraid to be called crazy, witnesses did not put the events on any official report. But as is in every case, a tale this big has a habit of leaking out. Many stories were shared when the soldiers returned from the battlefield. Some took the story to their graves.

Myles and Franz did return home safely to their families. How their life journeys ended I will leave to your imagination.

The End.

EPILOGUE

World War I lasted more than four years. It caused horrific bloodshed and the loss of around forty million lives, both military and civilian. My goal with this book was to immerse you in this time period. There are lessons and truths from this Great War that need to be remembered if we would only listen. We must learn from history, particularly the mistakes. Let's not let history be a cloud that simply moves away. If we can learn from the mistakes of the past, we can better mankind and one day maybe end war. Perhaps man is destined never to listen and occasional miracles and signs on the battlefields must occur to show us the way.

The final hours of the war are a lesson that must be shared. The Great War ended with an armistice signed at 5 a.m. on the 11th day of the 11th month of 1918, to seize on the 11th hour. With the knowledge of the war ending, the weapons at the Western Front did not fall silent till the last minute. This was pure selfishness by the command of both sides. It is my opinion that continuing the war till the last minute fits the definition of murder. The governments involved had a desire and not the necessity to slay the enemy.

Most historians tell us that the U.S. Army arrived too late on the Western Front to affect the war's outcome, an outcome determined by Allied grit, better tactics, the British blockade of German ports, and, ultimately, German exhaustion and revolution. The truth is the French and British were stalled in their sectors and barely hanging on in 1918. The faltering of the French and British could not have come at a worse moment. After the Germans had crushed the Russians and Italians, they began deploying 100 fresh divisions to the Western Front for a war-winning offensive that same year.

The American arrival, although late, was pivotal in turning defeat into victory. Especially when they took an offensive role. Starting September 26, 1918, after the greatest artillery bombardment in U.S. history, more shells in a few hours than had been fired in the entire American Civil War, 350,000 American soldiers advanced across no-man's-land toward the German trenches in the Meuse-Argonne offensive. They never stopped advancing, smashing through the Germans for 47 days until the armistice.

You may have noticed there is a relationship lesson in this book. I confess as the story developed I did not see it coming. The first known example of the proverb "All's fair in love and war" is from the English writer and courtier John Lyly's romantic novel *Euphues*: *The Anatomy of Wyt*, 1578, which says *"Anye impietie may lawfully be committed in love, which is lawlesse."* I may be one of the least qualified to teach on this subject but I have some experience.

Relationships can be a battle. All relationships have their challenges, and the strongest of relationships have weathered storms that could have torn them apart. While love, dedication, and hard work are essential to building a successful one, you must first have a strong foundation. Choosing the right person is a crucial first step in building a foundation that will withstand the test of time. Men and women are very different. Those differences exist so that each of you will balance the other out, but if you are unprepared to embrace those differences, it can strain even a healthy relationship.

I want you to decide for yourself whether miracles on the battlefield have occurred. If you research the matter, there is plenty of evidence to support supernatural intervention in war. Five months into the Great War a Christmas miracle did happen. This is a fact well documented. Parties of men from both sides began to venture toward the barbed wire that separated them, literally hundreds from each side were out in No Man's Land shaking hands. There is evidence of Tommy playing against Fritz in football matches. They saw the games as a bit of fun rather than a symbol of a futile war. Unfortunately, this Christmas miracle was not enough to stop the fighting. Both sides returned to their trenches with their views on the war unchanged and resumed fighting within a few days. Evidence supporting the miracle of the white cavalry is based on the story of what took place on a slight rise outside the town of Bethune, France. There are eyewitness reports and articles on the subject.

Perhaps the biggest miracle given to man is our ability to love. Although love is invisible, it is a powerful force. The power of love transcends time, distance, and space. As a child, we may first learn of it through our parents. Regardless of whether we learn it or not, it is in our hearts. We have only to listen and follow. Love is never lost, we can trust it to be real. It may be the only real miracle in a mostly dark universe.

SOURCES

Sacco, John. *The Great War: July 1, 1916: The first day of the Battle of the Somme*. WW Norton & Co 2013

Dash, Mike. "World War 1: 100 years later. The story of the WW1 Christmas Truce." Smithsonian Magazine SMITHSONIANMAG.COM 2011

Pearce, Dr. E Victor K. *Miracles & Angels*. Eagle Publishing 2002

Wall, Alexander J. "Preface," World War History: Daily Records and Comments as Appeared in American and Foreign Newspapers, 1914-1926. Compiled by Otto Spengler. NY: New-York Historical Society, 1928.

Imperial War Museum "Voices of the First World War," United Kingdom.ww.ivm.org.us/history/voices-of-the-first-war-arrival-of-the american-troops

The Attorney-General of the Government of Israel v. Adolf Eichmann, Minutes of Session No. 14, Jerusalem, 1961.

Countless original WW1 letters from soldiers to inspire the letters written in this book.

Also from this author:

THE FAITH
OF A CENTURION

CLEAN
FORGOTTEN
PATRIOTS

IN THE AMERICAN WAR
OF INDEPENDENCE

Available on Amazon
and Barnes & Noble.

www.ingramcontent.com/pod-product-compliance
Lightning Source LLC
Chambersburg PA
CBHW070115030726
47506CB00002B/758